WITHIN VENGANCE A TALE OF PRETENCE

SHE'LL HAVE TO PROTECT THEM FIRST—
EVEN IF IT MEANS RISKING HER OWN LIFE TO DO IT.

A book by
CHARLES MCCONAGHY

Copyright © 2025.

All rights reserved. No part of this book may be used or reproduced in any form whatsoever without written permission except in the case of brief quotations in critical articles or reviews.

All names, characters, businesses, organizations, places, events, and incidents are either products of the author's imagination or are used fictitiously. Any resemblance to real persons, living or deceased, actual events, or real locations is purely coincidental.

Printed in the United States of America.

With its sharp psychological tension and claustrophobic setting, *Within Vengeance* delivers a fresh twist on the classic revenge narrative. Perfect for fans of *Murder on the Orient Express* and *Gone Girl*, it's a dark, pulse-pounding ride that asks: how far would you go for justice—and who might die along the way

PREAMBLE

This book is dedicated to the unwavering spirits who have faced adversity with resilience, to those who have sought justice in the face of unimaginable loss, and to the quiet strength found in the human heart amidst chaos. It is a testament to the enduring power of hope, even in the darkest of times, and a recognition of the complexities that lie within the pursuit of revenge and the elusive nature of true justice. For those who have known the chilling grip of betrayal, the agonizing weight of grief, and the burning desire for retribution, may this story serve as a reflection of your own inner strength and the capacity to survive even the most harrowing of circumstances. To the unsung heroes who navigate the treacherous waters of moral ambiguity, striving to balance right and wrong in a world far from black and white, this narrative is a tribute to your quiet courage and unwavering determination.

To the women who refuse to be silenced, who stand tall in the face of adversity, and who seek to reclaim their power, this book is for you. May your resilience inspire generations to come. This dedication extends to those who find themselves caught in the crossfire of circumstance, forced to make impossible choices and navigate the treacherous landscape of life's unexpected turns. May your strength illuminate the path forward, reminding you that even in the deepest darkness, a glimmer of hope persists. The fight for justice is often a solitary one, fraught with peril and uncertainty, yet it is a fight worth undertaking, a testament to the indomitable spirit that resides within each of us. This dedication echoes the echoes of countless voices who have fought for what is right, who have faced down fear and uncertainty, who have emerged from the ashes of devastation, and who have found the strength to rebuild their lives.

This book is a dedication to the enduring power of the human spirit, to the resilience of those who have suffered, and to the unwavering pursuit of a better tomorrow, even when the path is fraught with obstacles and uncertainty. It is a tribute to the quiet strength found within us all, a strength that enables us to navigate the complexities of life, to endure unimaginable loss, and to ultimately emerge stronger and more determined. For those who have faced the abyss and emerged victorious, this story is an acknowledgement of your courage, your resilience, and your unwavering belief in the possibility of hope. May this book resonate with those who have sought justice, even when the path is fraught with moral ambiguity, those who have endured hardship and persevered despite the overwhelming odds, and those who have discovered the power of their own inner strength to overcome even the greatest of challenges.

Chapter 1
The Setup

The rain hammered against the panoramic windows of Ava's apartment, mirroring the relentless storm raging inside her. The city lights blurred into streaks of neon, a chaotic backdrop to the meticulous order of her workspace. Files overflowed from meticulously labelled boxes, each one containing a meticulously gathered piece of the puzzle she'd spent the last two years assembling. Photographs, financial records, travel itineraries – a tapestry woven from the lives of four men who had shattered hers.

Ava traced a finger across a photograph, her touch feather-light on the smiling faces of her parents. The image, a relic from a happier time, now served as a stark reminder of the devastation she carried within. The accident, deemed a tragic mishap, was a carefully constructed lie, a conspiracy woven by the powerful and ruthless. And Ava, armed with an arsenal of intellect and a burning thirst for vengeance, was determined to unravel it.

She wasn't driven by rage, not in the raw, uncontrolled sense. Her fury was refined, honed to a surgical precision. Grief fueled her, but it was a cold, calculating grief, sharpened by the injustice that had stolen everything from her. It was a grief that propelled her through countless sleepless nights, driving her to master surveillance techniques, decipher encrypted communications, and manipulate legal loopholes. She'd become a ghost, a phantom navigating the city's underbelly, always one step ahead, always unseen.

Ava's apartment was a testament to her methodical approach. Every detail was precisely placed, every item had a purpose. This wasn't a haven, but a command center, an arsenal of information waiting to be deployed. A wall-sized whiteboard displayed a complex network of interconnected names, dates, and locations – a visual representation of the conspiracy she was dismantling. Red threads linked the four men at the heart of her plot: Arthur Blackwood, the ruthless CEO; Julian Thorne, the ambitious lawyer; Marcus Davies, the corrupt politician; and finally, Reginald Hayes, the silent partner, whose influence was far-reaching and shadowy.

Each man had played a crucial role in the orchestrated accident that killed her parents, an accident conveniently dismissed as a tragic accident. Ava knew the truth, though, each piece of evidence, painstakingly gathered, solidified her conviction. She wouldn't rest until they faced the consequences of their actions, until justice, however she defined it, was served. Justice that the law, with its labyrinthine processes and ingrained biases, would never deliver.

Her gaze fell upon a sleek, silver laptop open on her desk. The screen displayed a detailed itinerary for the 10:00 AM Philadelphia-bound express train. This was her chessboard, and the four men were her pawns. They were all travelling together, a fortuitous coincidence she had subtly orchestrated. An exclusive corporate retreat, a seamlessly woven lie that had lured them into her trap. The luxurious train, a symbol of their wealth and power, would become their gilded cage.

A faint tremor of vulnerability, a fleeting crack in her carefully constructed facade, appeared. A single tear escaped, tracing a path down her cheek. It was a rare glimpse into the woman buried beneath the architect of revenge, a woman still haunted by the memory of her parents' laughter, their warmth, their unwavering love. She quickly wiped it away, her expression returning to its usual mask of icy determination. The game was about to begin.

The meticulously planned schedule of the day danced before her eyes; a coordinated dance of arrival times, precise locations, and subtle distractions. She had accounted for every variable, anticipated every contingency. Her targets were confident, arrogant, oblivious to the impending doom they were speeding toward. The meticulously planned ambush was in place, poised and ready. The city outside continued to rage, a symphony of thunder and rain that matched the storm brewing within her.

Ava's apartment, despite its carefully arranged contents, had a strange sense of stillness. The absence of any emotional clutter was almost unsettling. It felt as though the very walls held their breath, anticipating the execution of her perfectly formed plan. It was a space where silence screamed louder than any shouting match. This wasn't just an apartment; it was the nerve center of a meticulous revenge plot, and the heart of a woman driven by loss and a burning need to find balance in the face of a cruelly unbalanced world.

As the clock ticked closer to 9:30 AM, Ava began her preparations, moving with a practiced efficiency. She checked her equipment one last time – a sophisticated listening device, a compact high-resolution camera disguised as a pen, and a small but powerful transmitter hidden beneath her coat. Everything was in place. Her movements were almost balletic, each step deliberate, measured, devoid of any hint of nervousness. She was a predator stalking its prey, patiently waiting for the opportune moment to strike.

The train's opulence was a deliberate choice. The opulent carriages, the gleaming silverware, the impeccable service – it was all part of the bait. The four men, accustomed to such luxury, would feel entirely at ease. Their complacency would be their undoing. The train's route was another key element of Ava's plan. The journey would take them through remote stretches of Pennsylvania countryside, far from prying eyes and help. The train was a self-contained universe, perfectly suited for her carefully crafted chaos.

The meticulously crafted narrative she had woven would now begin to unfurl. The weight of her plan, the burden of her grief, was a heavy cloak, but it was also a source of strength, a catalyst for the chilling precision of her actions. Ava glanced at the mirror, adjusting her coat. The woman staring back was a stranger, a reflection of the cold calculation that had become her shield. Yet, behind the steely gaze, a spark of sorrow flickered – a testament to the devastating loss that had ignited this relentless pursuit of justice. The rain outside intensified, but inside, Ava's focus remained unwavering. The game was set; it was time to play.

The Philadelphia-bound express train hissed into the station, a metallic serpent slithering into the heart of the city. Ava watched from a discreet vantage point across the platform, her silhouette a mere shadow against the rain-streaked glass of a nearby coffee shop. Binoculars, cleverly disguised as a pair of expensive sunglasses, were trained on the boarding passengers. Her targets were easy to spot: Arthur Blackwood, his tailored suit impeccably pressed, exuded an air of arrogant confidence; Julian Thorne, a picture of slick ambition, chatted animatedly on his phone, oblivious to the storm brewing around him; Marcus Davies, the politician, attempted a casual demeanor, but his eyes darted nervously, betraying his inner turmoil. Reginald Hayes, the silent partner, remained an enigma, his face obscured by the wide brim of his hat, his movements deliberately subdued, yet radiating an undeniable aura of power.

Ava's heart hammered against her ribs, a counterpoint to the rhythmic chugging of the train. This was it. The culmination of two years of meticulous planning, of sleepless nights spent poring over documents, of navigating treacherous social circles and exploiting legal loopholes. It wasn't just a revenge scheme; it was a symphony of calculated moves, a masterpiece of strategic deception, all orchestrated to expose the four men responsible for her family's destruction.

A flashback ripped through her mind. The blinding flash of headlights, the screech of tires, the sickening crunch of metal. The image of her parents' car, mangled and twisted, seared itself onto her memory. The subsequent investigation, hampered by official incompetence and outright corruption, had only confirmed her suspicions. The accident, ruled a tragic mishap, was a carefully staged assassination. These four men, powerful and interconnected, had erased her family with calculated precision, leaving no trace except for the gaping hole they'd left in her life.

The scene shifted back to the present. Ava watched as the four men settled into their first-class compartment, their laughter echoing through the cavernous space. Their unawareness was almost comical; the irony wasn't lost on Ava. They believed themselves untouchable, secure in their wealth and influence. They were the puppeteers, pulling the strings of a corrupt system, yet utterly unaware of the invisible hand controlling them now.

The opulent interior of the train was a stark contrast to the darkness fueling Ava's mission. Plush velvet seating, gleaming mahogany paneling, crystal glasses, silver cutlery – a world of extravagant luxury that felt alien to her now. She remembered a time when such opulence represented freedom, security, a family life untouched by tragedy. Now, it only served as a symbol of their power, their arrogance, their impunity.

Ava's camera pen, cleverly concealed in her hand, captured every detail, every exchange, every careless comment. The transmitter tucked away beneath her coat relayed everything to her laptop back at her apartment, where an AI program was diligently transcribing, analyzing, and building a case. This train was not just a vessel; it was a mobile courtroom, and Ava was the unseen judge, jury, and executioner.

Arthur Blackwood, the CEO, seemed to be enjoying his power, orchestrating a business deal with casual confidence. His voice, amplified by the sophisticated listening device Ava had planted, filled her ears. He spoke of mergers, of acquisitions, of manipulating markets – the casual callousness mirroring the way he had manipulated events to erase her parents. Julian Thorne, the lawyer, added his expertise, discussing the legal intricacies of shady transactions. His words were a tapestry of carefully chosen terms and loopholes that underscored the systemic corruption he participated in, his complicity with Blackwood's machinations.

Marcus Davies, the politician, sat nervously, his usual bravado overshadowed by his apprehension. Ava had discovered a series of compromising documents implicating him in a money-laundering scheme, a discovery that served as one of her strongest weapons.

His attempts at concealing his discomfort spoke louder than any confession. He knew the truth about the accident, his role in the cover-up. But his fear was not for his actions but for the exposure of his secrets.

Reginald Hayes remained an enigma, even amidst the cacophony of conversation. He said little, observed much, his eyes, as dark and profound as the depths of Ava's grief, seemed to pierce through every facade of deception. His silent presence was more powerful than any overt act; he was the unseen hand, pulling the strings from the shadows.

Ava observed their interactions, a predator studying its prey. Their laughter seemed hollow to her, their casual cruelty a reminder of the devastation they had wrought. The train, a symbol of their privileged world, was rapidly becoming their prison. Their obliviousness to the growing danger was a constant source of dark amusement to Ava. It was the complacency that fueled her mission. It was a complacency born of unchecked power, of a belief in their absolute immunity.

The train continued its journey, hurtling through the Pennsylvania countryside. The landscape outside the windows became a blur of green hills and rushing rivers;

a picture of serene beauty that was utterly at odds with the storm of vengeance brewing inside the train. Ava shifted her focus to the various security cameras strategically placed throughout the train's interior. Her eyes danced across the surveillance monitors displaying high-resolution footage, her gaze sharp and focused.

She'd even accounted for the possibility of them bringing bodyguards, which turned out to be accurate. Two burly men, dressed in discreet suits, were assigned to protect Blackwood and Hayes. Ava had already incorporated the presence of these two bodyguards into her plans. She planned to use this situation to her advantage, creating an atmosphere of disorientation and chaos, thereby giving her the leverage to execute her plan.

A sharp intake of breath escaped Ava's lips as she observed an exchange between Blackwood and Hayes. They seemed to be discussing some critical issue, the gravity of their conversation evident in their guarded tones. Ava's mind raced; she needed to get a better idea of what was being discussed, but they were speaking in hushed tones. This was the moment to put her enhanced listening device to good use.

She adjusted her position, her hand moving with a fluid, practiced grace. With a deft movement, she activated the advanced microphone hidden in her pen. This microphone could amplify the faintest sounds, ensuring that she could intercept their conversation without raising any suspicion. The voices of Blackwood and Hayes filled her ears, faint at first, but gradually becoming clearer. The details that emerged from their hushed conversation would prove to be pivotal in her quest for revenge. This was the kind of crucial information that would help her dismantle their entire operation.

The train was her stage, and Ava, the invisible director, was carefully controlling the narrative of its final act. The game, she knew, was far from over. The next few hours would determine the fate of these four men, and the fate of her own long-awaited justice. The weight of her vengeance was a heavy burden, yet it was a weight she carried with a steely resolve. The rain continued to fall, a constant, rhythmic reminder of the tears she had shed, and the tears she was yet to cry.

The rhythmic clatter of the train wheels against the tracks was a hypnotic counterpoint to the simmering tension within the first-class carriage. Ava, concealed behind a pillar near the observation car, watched as the four men—Blackwood, Thorne, Davies, and Hayes—

continued their seemingly innocuous conversation. Their obliviousness to the danger brewing was both infuriating and darkly amusing. She had underestimated one factor, however: the unexpected passengers.

A subtle shift in the atmosphere, almost imperceptible at first, alerted Ava to their presence. A low murmur, a barely audible shift in the collective hum of the train, signaled something was amiss. It wasn't the usual chatter of first-class passengers; this was different, colder, sharper. It was the sound of predators amongst the prey.

Her eyes, honed by years of meticulous observation, scanned the carriage. She spotted them then, seated near the rear, blending seamlessly into the opulence. They looked like any other corporate executives; impeccably dressed, their faces carefully neutral. But Ava recognized the subtle signs: the way they held themselves, the almost imperceptible tension in their shoulders, the sharp angles of their jaws, the predatory gleam in their eyes. These were not businessmen; these were wolves in tailored suits.

Their leader sat apart, a woman named Seraphina Moreau. Unlike her companions, she didn't attempt to blend in. She was striking, almost beautiful, with piercing grey eyes that seemed to see everything, know everything. Her tailored black suit was severe, her demeanor commanding, radiating an icy aura that froze the air around her. She didn't speak much, but when she did, her voice was a low, silken whisper that cut through the train's ambient noise like a knife.

Ava's initial assessment was that these were not typical criminals. They operated with a chilling efficiency, a quiet professionalism that suggested meticulous planning and a high level of expertise. This wasn't a spontaneous hijacking; this was a meticulously crafted operation.

The realization struck Ava with the force of a physical blow. Her meticulously crafted plan was now compromised. She had anticipated the reactions of her targets; she had planned for various contingencies. But she hadn't foreseen this. The intrusion of this criminal element had thrown everything into disarray.

The unexpected passengers' plan became evident as the train left the station. Their leader, Seraphina Moreau, issued barely audible instructions to her team. Their targets weren't just the four men Ava sought to expose; they were all the wealthy passengers aboard the train. This was a high-stakes robbery, a carefully orchestrated heist designed to exploit the train's isolated environment. The initial interactions between Seraphina's team and Ava's targets were tense, filled with an underlying current of menace. One of Seraphina's men, a large, imposing figure named Dmitri, casually bumped into Arthur Blackwood, spilling his drink. The apology was perfunctory, the touch lingering, a subtle display of power. Blackwood, initially annoyed, brushed it off, oblivious to the danger he was in.

Another member of the group, a woman with sharp features and a deceptively sweet smile, engaged Julian Thorne in conversation. Her charm was disarming, her questions deceptively innocent. But Ava saw the calculating glint in her eyes, the subtle manipulation as she subtly gathered information about Thorne's movements, his patterns.

The tension escalated as the train gained speed. The Pennsylvania countryside raced past the windows, a hypnotic blur of green and brown. But inside, the atmosphere was thick with unspoken threats, a silent war brewing beneath the surface of polite conversation.

Ava realised she had to adapt. Her plan was no longer about exposing the four men; it was about survival. The criminals posed a significant threat, not just to her targets, but to all the passengers, including herself. Her meticulously gathered evidence was still valuable, but it was secondary now to the immediate and pressing danger.

Seraphina's team was working methodically, using a combination of intimidation and subtle manipulation. They were identifying valuable targets, assessing security measures, laying the groundwork for the heist. Ava watched, analyzing their movements, their strategies. She was forced to improvise, to shift her focus from a meticulously planned revenge to a desperate fight for survival.

The situation was far more complex than she had anticipated. The line between victim and perpetrator was blurring, the roles of all players shifting with every passing moment. She was no longer simply an instrument of revenge; she was a pawn in a larger game, a dangerous game played by criminals far more ruthless than she had ever imagined.

The train journey, once a meticulously planned path to justice, had become a chaotic battlefield, a claustrophobic space where every moment held the potential for violence, betrayal, and death. The seemingly innocuous passengers were now potential victims, and her targets were no longer the sole focus of her attention. The weight of her mission was compounded by the sudden realization of her new position in this deadly game of chance.

The next few hours would be a test not only of her cunning and resolve, but also of her adaptability and survival instincts. She was no longer the orchestrator of a symphony of revenge; she was now a participant in a deadly dance, her fate intertwined with that of the other passengers, including her original targets. The train, once her instrument, was now a prison, a high-speed coffin hurtling towards an uncertain future.

The opulent surroundings of the first-class carriage, once symbols of the wealth and power she sought to dismantle, now served as a stark backdrop to the looming chaos. The plush velvet seats, the gleaming mahogany paneling, the crystal glasses—all were silent witnesses to the escalating tension, the growing threat.

The rhythmic chugging of the train served as a constant reminder of their inescapable predicament. With every passing mile, the threat grew, the tension mounted, the possibility of violence becoming increasingly palpable. Ava knew that the coming confrontation would be brutal, a test of her strength, her resilience, and her ability to survive against overwhelming odds. The game had changed, but her determination remained unwavering. She would fight. She had to. Her family's memory demanded nothing less. Justice, however, might need to wait. Survival was now the priority. The train hurtled forward, a runaway vessel carrying a volatile mix of victims and predators, all hurtling towards a destination none of them could predict. The unexpected passengers had turned the planned revenge into a fight for survival, a deadly game with unimaginable stakes. And Ava, the initially unseen director, was now just another player in this high-stakes gamble.

The initial, almost imperceptible shift in the train's rhythm intensified into a full-blown assault. Seraphina Moreau, her face devoid of emotion, gave a barely perceptible nod. The transformation was instantaneous. Dmitri, the imposing figure, moved with the speed and precision of a trained assassin, his large frame surprisingly agile as he swept through the carriage. He didn't shout or brandish a weapon; his mere presence was enough to cow most passengers into submission. His movements were economical, efficient, practiced. He subdued several passengers with swift, expertly placed strikes, their surprised gasps swallowed by the relentless roar of the train.

Simultaneously, the other members of Seraphina's team sprang into action. The woman with the deceptively sweet smile, whose name Ava later learned was Irina, worked with chilling efficiency, her seemingly innocent demeanor a perfect camouflage for her brutal effectiveness. She moved through the carriage like a phantom, disarming passengers with a practiced ease that belied her delicate frame. Her weapon of choice wasn't a gun, but a small, almost invisible device that emitted a high-pitched frequency, causing temporary disorientation and incapacitation.

Chaos erupted. Screams were cut short by the deafening sound of the train, the cries of the terrified passengers swallowed by the relentless rhythm of the steel wheels. Ava, momentarily stunned by the sudden violence, quickly recovered her composure. Her carefully crafted plan was in tatters, but her survival instincts kicked in. Years of training and meticulous planning served her now not in the execution of her original revenge scheme, but in a desperate fight for survival.

She pressed herself closer against the pillar, observing the unfolding scene with a clinical eye. She needed to assess the situation, to identify vulnerabilities, to formulate a new plan. The train was a steel cage hurtling down the tracks, a prison where escape was impossible, where the predators and prey were inextricably intertwined. The carefully cultivated opulence of the first-class carriage now served as a grotesque backdrop to the unfolding horror.

The initial shock gave way to a chilling clarity. Seraphina's team was not interested in ransom; this was not a typical hijacking. This was a highly organized operation, with precision and efficiency that spoke of extensive planning and experience. Their targets were not just the passengers, but something far more valuable: the contents of their luggage, the jewels, the cash, the seemingly innocuous items containing fortunes hidden in plain sight.

The methodical precision of the criminals' actions unnerved Ava. It was calculated, almost surgical in its efficiency. Every move, every glance, every word spoke of an almost ruthless intelligence at play. They were not driven by greed alone, it appeared; there was a cold, calculated purpose behind this act that went beyond mere material gain.

Ava, utilizing the shadows and the ensuing chaos, moved stealthily, keeping a low profile while observing Seraphina and her crew. She noted the precise way in which Dmitri dealt with resistance, the subtle techniques used by Irina to disarm and subdue the passengers, the quiet efficiency with which the other two members of the group secured valuables. This wasn't random violence; it was controlled, measured, and ruthlessly efficient.

The claustrophobic nature of the speeding train amplified the sense of danger. Every scream, every thud, every rustle resonated within the confines of the carriage, creating a symphony of fear and desperation. The plush velvet seats, the polished mahogany, the sparkling crystal – all served as stark reminders of the wealth being plundered from the helpless passengers.

Ava's initial plan had been meticulously crafted, a carefully laid trap aimed at exposing the four men responsible for her family's ruin. Now, that plan lay in pieces. But she wasn't ready to surrender. Her training, honed over years of covert operations, kicked into high gear. She needed to recalculate, to adapt, to survive.

She studied Seraphina, the leader of the hijackers. Seraphina commanded authority with an icy calm that sent shivers down Ava's spine. Her gaze was sharp, calculating, never missing a detail. The way she delegated tasks, the almost imperceptible signals she sent to her team, spoke volumes of her experience and command. This wasn't merely a crime; it was a well-orchestrated ballet of brutality.

The situation shifted dramatically. Ava was no longer the hunter; she was now the hunted, a pawn in a much larger, far more dangerous game. Her initial anger and desire for revenge were now superseded by the primal need for survival. The fight for justice had turned into a struggle for life itself. The train, once a vessel for her plan, was now a death trap, hurtling towards an uncertain destination, carrying a cargo of victims and predators, all caught in a web of chaos and violence.

Ava realized that to survive, she needed to understand Seraphina's ultimate goal. What was she truly after? Was it the money? The jewels? Or was there something more sinister at play? The questions swirled in Ava's mind as she made her way to a less-crowded part of the car, her mind working furiously. She needed to gain an advantage, to find a weakness in Seraphina's seemingly impenetrable plan. She was a chess player now, forced to adapt to a different game entirely, one in which the stakes were not justice, but survival itself. The clock was ticking, and every second brought them closer to an uncertain, deadly destination. The train screamed along the tracks, a metal beast consuming the distance, and carrying with it a volatile mix of terrified passengers and ruthlessly efficient criminals. Ava, once in control, was now a player reacting to a master plan far beyond her own design. The future was uncertain, and survival was her only priority. The ride to Philadelphia had become a fight for life itself.

The rhythmic clatter of the train, a relentless percussion against the backdrop of escalating panic, was almost a welcome distraction from the chilling efficiency of Seraphina's team. Ava, concealed behind a tattered tapestry, watched as a wiry, older gentleman, initially cowering under a seat, began to meticulously dismantle a small, antique music box. His hands, gnarled and trembling, moved with surprising dexterity, revealing a hidden compartment containing a small, intricately designed device. It looked like a sophisticated communication device, far beyond anything a casual traveler would possess.

This wasn't a random act of pilfering; this was a calculated diversion. The man, whom Ava had initially dismissed as another terrified passenger, was clearly far more than that. His actions, precise and deliberate, suggested a level of knowledge and preparation that defied his frail appearance. He glanced towards Ava, his eyes betraying a flicker of intelligence, a silent acknowledgment of shared danger.

Across the carriage, a young woman with fiery red hair and a defiant glare – someone Ava had recognized from the passenger manifest as Eleanor Vance, one of the supposed corporate executives on her list – was engaging Dmitri in a silent, intense standoff. Dmitri, towering over her, clearly underestimated her. Eleanor, despite her petite frame, exuded an unwavering strength. Her expression, a mixture of fear and defiance, hinted at a hidden strength, a capacity for violence that belied her initial appearance.

Suddenly, Eleanor made a move, swift and unexpected. She kicked out, connecting with Dmitri's leg with surprising force, causing him to stumble. It was a desperate gamble, but it worked. Before Dmitri could regain his balance, the older gentleman, his disassembly of the music box complete, activated the device. A high-pitched whine filled the air, momentarily disorienting Dmitri and his two accomplices. In the resulting confusion, Eleanor seized an opportunity, grabbing a heavy, ornate lamp and using it to disable one of the hijackers.

The unexpected intervention changed the dynamics of the situation. It wasn't just Seraphina's team versus the passengers anymore. It was a chaotic scramble for survival, a ballet of violence and desperation played out in the cramped confines of the speeding train. Ava realized she couldn't rely solely on her initial plan; she needed allies. Allies she hadn't anticipated, allies she would have previously dismissed as victims.

The older gentleman, surprisingly agile despite his age, moved with a grace that belied his initial appearance of fragility. He whispered to Ava, his voice raspy but firm, "They're after more than money. The device... it's a disruptor. They're trying to silence someone, someone powerful."

Eleanor, despite being wounded, continued to fight, her courage inspiring other passengers. A burly man, initially paralyzed by fear, now helped her fend off another of Seraphina's henchmen, surprising everyone with his unexpected strength and determination. The alliances were fluid, temporary, forged in the crucible of shared fear and desperate hope.

The train hurtled towards Philadelphia, each passing mile adding urgency to their desperate fight. The initial chaos was slowly giving way to an uneasy equilibrium, a precarious balance between the hijackers' control and the passengers' growing defiance. Ava watched, assessing, calculating. She had to figure out how to use this newfound, unexpected cooperation to her advantage.

The older gentleman, whom she now learned was named Professor Alistair Finch, a renowned cryptographer, explained that the disruptor was designed to disable a specific type of secure communication system, one he suspected was being used by a powerful organization. His own work had made him a target, which was why he was on the train, disguised and equipped to counter the disruptor's effects.

Eleanor, recovering from her injury, revealed that she wasn't a corporate executive but an undercover agent working for a rival organization. Her assignment had brought her face to face with the very men Seraphina had targeted – the men who had destroyed Ava's family, and whom she, in turn, had planned to expose. Eleanor, initially caught in the crosshairs of Ava's vengeful plan, had now become an unexpected ally. Her knowledge of Seraphina's organization, coupled with the Professor's technical expertise, offered Ava a chance to not only survive but to finally achieve her goal – but on vastly different terms than she had initially envisioned.

The dynamic shifted again. Ava, no longer alone, now had two unexpected accomplices working alongside her. Each brought unique skills and experience to the table, transforming the fight from a desperate struggle for survival into a carefully choreographed battle against a formidable enemy.

The trust among this unlikely alliance was fragile, built on shared danger and mutual need. Ava sensed a degree of skepticism in both the Professor and Eleanor, but their shared enemy and their shared proximity in this metal death trap were proving stronger than suspicion. The fact that they were now united against Seraphina's ruthless operation, each with a common interest in foiling her scheme, forced them to cooperate.

However, underneath the surface of their newfound cooperation, a simmering tension persisted. The Professor's reticence about his past, his almost furtive glances, hinted at a more complex story than the one he had revealed. Eleanor's relentless, almost ruthless efficiency, her cold calculation, suggested a professional detachment that kept Ava at arm's length. Ava knew they were united in this moment of crisis, but the true nature of their alliances and their individual motivations remained a mystery.

As the train rattled closer to its destination, the weight of uncertainty pressed down. The initial plan had disintegrated, replaced by a fluid, evolving conflict where the lines between victim and predator were perpetually shifting. Ava understood that to succeed in this new reality, she needed to navigate the intricate web of alliances and betrayals, trust her new allies strategically, and exploit the weaknesses of her enemies. The journey to Philadelphia was no longer a simple revenge mission; it had become a high-stakes game of survival, deception, and unexpected partnerships, where the final outcome remained uncertain until the very last moment. The question wasn't just who would survive, but who would emerge victorious in this deadly game of cat and mouse. The journey to Philadelphia had become a crucible forging a desperate alliance; an alliance forged in the fires of a hijacked train, hurtling towards its inevitable, potentially fatal, destination.

Chapter 2
Shifting Sands

The air in the cramped communications room hung thick with the metallic tang of fear and the stale scent of recycled air. Rain lashed against the train's windows, a relentless counterpoint to the rhythmic clatter of the wheels. Marco, one of Seraphina's men, sat hunched over a battered satellite phone, his face illuminated by the flickering screen's sickly green glow. He was the designated negotiator, his role thrust upon him by the chaotic turn of events. His initial swagger had been replaced by a nervous twitch in his left eye, a stark contrast to the cold calculation usually present in his demeanour.

Ava watched him from the shadows, her heart a frantic drum against her ribs. She'd followed him here, using the confusion and the desperate scramble for safety as cover. Her initial plan—a meticulously crafted revenge scheme—lay in ruins, shattered by the unexpected hijacking. Now, her focus had shifted to survival, and to gathering information, any information, that could help her turn the tide. Marco was her key.

His voice, when he spoke, was a low, gravelly murmur, barely audible above the train's cacophony. He was talking to the authorities, or at least, that's what he claimed. Ava couldn't hear the other side of the conversation, but she observed the subtle shifts in his posture, the barely perceptible clenching of his jaw, the fleeting moments of doubt that clouded his usually steely gaze. He wasn't just relaying demands; he was playing a game, a complex dance of deception that made her skin crawl.

"They want... assurances," he muttered, his voice barely a whisper. He glanced towards the door, his eyes darting nervously. He was acutely aware of his precarious position, balancing precariously on the edge of a knife. One wrong move, one slip, and the whole charade could collapse, leaving him exposed.

Ava focused on his words, trying to decipher the truth hidden within the carefully crafted lies. "Assurances of what?" she whispered back, her voice barely audible.

Marco jumped, whirling around, his hand instinctively reaching for the pistol tucked into his waistband. His eyes, wide with surprise and a flicker of something akin to panic, scanned the cramped space. He relaxed slightly when he saw it was only Ava. There was a fleeting moment of recognition, a shared understanding of their shared predicament, however fleeting.

"They want proof," he rasped, his voice tight with barely contained tension. "Proof that we're not going to harm the passengers. Proof that we'll release them." His words were laced with a cynical undertone, a hint of disbelief in the very assurances he was offering.

Ava's mind raced. This wasn't just a simple hostage situation; this was a carefully orchestrated maneuver, far more intricate than she could have initially imagined. She needed to understand Marco's motivations, his loyalties, and the extent of his involvement. Was he truly negotiating for the release of the hostages, or was he playing a far more dangerous game?

She feigned ignorance, playing her own role in this deadly charade. "And what are you offering them?" she asked, her voice carefully neutral, devoid of any emotion that might betray her thoughts.

Marco paused, seemingly lost in thought. He ran a hand through his already disheveled hair, his face a mask of weariness and barely-contained frustration. "A show of good faith," he mumbled, his gaze drifting towards the door again. "A staged release... a few passengers." He hesitated, then added, almost as an afterthought, "But the key players...they stay."

Ava's stomach twisted. He was talking about the others—Seraphina and her inner circle. He was using the hostages as bargaining chips, a human sacrifice to protect their true targets. His actions, she was now certain, were less than genuine. He was negotiating but clearly, not wholeheartedly on behalf of his own team.

The next few minutes were a blur of intense tension. Marco, torn between his loyalty to his accomplices and a growing sense of self-preservation, engaged in a desperate battle of wills with the authorities. His negotiations became a cat-and-mouse game of calculated risks and veiled threats. He offered concessions, only to retract them at the last moment, creating a dangerous spiral of uncertainty. His very actions seemed to feed the chaos unfolding. He appeared to be creating a more dangerous situation, testing the waters, feeling his way along.

Ava, meanwhile, meticulously observed his every move. She noted the subtle nuances of his body language, the almost imperceptible hesitations in his speech, the way his eyes flickered towards the door every few seconds. These were not the actions of a man wholeheartedly committed to his cause.

As he spoke, Ava gathered clues. She intercepted fragments of his conversation, gleaned information from his frustrated mutterings, and analyzed the very tone of his voice, which revealed cracks in his façade of ruthless efficiency. He was clearly more than simply a henchman; she suspected he had a hidden agenda, a personal stake in this game.

Marco's negotiations were fraught with uncertainty. Every word he spoke was weighed carefully, measured, calculated to achieve an unknown end. He seemed to be playing both sides, keeping the authorities at bay while subtly manipulating events to suit his own, still-unclear purpose.

As the minutes ticked by, the tension in the room became almost palpable. The rhythmic clatter of the train seemed to echo the frantic beat of Ava's heart. She knew that time was running out. Marco's game couldn't last forever. The authorities were getting impatient. Seraphina's patience was also wearing thin. The true test of Marco's loyalty, and Ava's own chances of survival, would come down to the wire. This was the moment where everything would hinge. This was the pivot upon which their fate rested.

The final moments of the negotiations were a whirlwind of frantic activity. Marco, his face pale and streaked with sweat, appeared to be on the verge of a complete breakdown. His carefully constructed façade was cracking under the relentless pressure. Ava's perception of Marco was evolving rapidly, her understanding of his true motives still obscured, but now seen with greater clarity.

He paced restlessly within the confines of the small communications room, his every action imbued with barely controlled anxiety. Suddenly, he stopped, a tremor running through him. He stared at Ava, his eyes filled with a complex mixture of fear and resignation. In a moment of surprising vulnerability, a desperate plea, he whispered a single word: "Help."

This seemingly insignificant word shifted everything. It was a tacit admission of failure, a silent acknowledgment of his own precarious position, and an unexpected invitation to cooperate. Ava knew now she had to make a choice, a choice that could not only determine the fate of the hostages, but that could seal her own destiny. The game, it seemed, had just begun anew, with a new, unexpected, and potentially lethal player joining the fray. The train roared closer to Philadelphia, its inexorable approach a constant reminder of the ticking clock.

The whispered word, "Help," hung in the air like a poisoned dart. Ava felt a cold dread seep into her bones, a chilling premonition that this seemingly simple plea masked a far more treacherous reality. Marco's sudden vulnerability was unsettling, a stark contrast to the calculating ruthlessness he'd displayed moments before. Had he truly broken, or was this a meticulously crafted deception, a new layer added to the intricate game he was playing?

She studied him, her gaze unwavering, searching for the glint of manipulation behind the mask of desperation. His eyes, usually steely and cold, were now dilated, reflecting a genuine fear that went beyond the immediate danger. He was sweating profusely, his breath coming in ragged gasps, a testament to the strain he was under. His usual composed demeanor was shattered, replaced by a raw vulnerability that was both unsettling and strangely compelling.

Ava considered her options. Trusting Marco was a gamble with potentially fatal consequences. He was a criminal, after all, and his motivations remained shrouded in mystery. Yet, ignoring his plea felt equally dangerous. He held vital information, information that could be the key to her survival, and possibly to the survival of the hostages. This was a high-stakes poker game, and every decision held the weight of life or death.

"What kind of help do you need?" she asked, her voice carefully neutral, devoid of any emotion that might give him an advantage. She kept her distance, her body language subtly defensive, ready to react to any sudden change in his demeanor. His betrayal of his own cohort had shaken the foundation of her plan; she couldn't afford another misstep.

Marco swallowed hard, his Adam's apple bobbing nervously. He glanced towards the door, then back at Ava, his gaze darting nervously. He seemed to be weighing his words, choosing them carefully, as if each syllable carried a hidden meaning.

"They... they're planning something," he finally whispered, his voice barely audible above the train's relentless clatter. "Something far worse than just holding the passengers hostage." His words were laced with a desperate urgency, a palpable fear that sent a shiver down Ava's spine.

"Worse?" Ava pressed, her voice low and urgent. "What do you mean?"

He hesitated, his eyes darting around the cramped room, as if fearing unseen eyes and ears. He leaned closer, his voice dropping to a near-inaudible murmur. "Seraphina... she has a secondary objective. The hostages are just a distraction."

Ava's mind raced, piecing together fragments of information. Seraphina's ruthless ambition had always been a known quantity, but this revelation added a layer of chilling complexity. The initial hijacking was just a smokescreen, a carefully orchestrated ruse to mask a far more sinister plan.

"What's her objective?" Ava demanded, her patience wearing thin. The train was hurtling closer to Philadelphia, the final destination, the climax of this terrifying journey, rapidly approaching. Every second counted.

Marco took a deep breath, seemingly gathering the courage to reveal a dangerous secret. "A package," he whispered, his voice tight with barely-contained fear. "A very valuable package. She's using the hostages to secure its safe passage."

The significance of his words struck Ava with the force of a physical blow. This wasn't just about revenge or power; it was about something far more valuable, something that could trigger a conflict of far greater magnitude. A package of this significance could be anything - a priceless artifact, a trove of classified data, or even a deadly bioweapon. The possibilities were horrifying.

The landscape outside the speeding train blurred into a frantic montage of Pennsylvania's countryside – rolling hills, scattered farmhouses, and the occasional fleeting glimpse of a small town. The tranquil beauty of the external world provided a stark contrast to the chaos that reigned within the confines of the train. The outside represented freedom, a world where the hostages could be and the perpetrators could be brought to justice, while inside was chaos.

The next few hours were a blur of intense activity. Marco, now an unlikely ally, provided Ava with crucial information. He revealed the location of the package, a hidden compartment beneath the train's baggage car. He also divulged Seraphina's plan – to transfer the package to a waiting accomplice at the Philadelphia station, using the chaos of the hostage situation as cover.

Ava, with Marco's help, rallied a small group of unwitting passengers—those who had demonstrated a spark of courage and resilience. They included a former military medic, a tech-savvy student, and a surprisingly strong elderly woman. They planned a daring counter-offensive – to seize control of the train, secure the package, and bring Seraphina and her accomplices to justice.

Their plan was risky, borderline suicidal. But it was their only hope. As the train hurtled closer to Philadelphia, the tension ratcheted up, a palpable sense of dread hanging over them. The game had shifted once more, the allegiances rewritten. The initial goal, Ava's personal revenge, was now secondary to preventing a catastrophe of unimaginable proportions.

The betrayal within Seraphina's group wasn't limited to Marco. One of Seraphina's closest confidants, a woman named Isabella, revealed a hidden agenda of her own. It turned out Isabella had been secretly working with the authorities, providing them with information in exchange for immunity. This revelation sent shockwaves through their fragile alliance. Trust, already a scarce commodity, dwindled even further.

Isabella's betrayal, however, provided a crucial advantage. She knew Seraphina's every move, her weaknesses, and her contingency plans. With Isabella's intel, Ava and her motley crew refined their strategy, increasing their chances of success. The shifting sands of loyalty and betrayal continued to reshape the landscape of the speeding train. It was a dangerous dance, played out amidst the confines of a metal serpent hurtling toward an uncertain future. Ava's mission had evolved; it was no longer just about revenge. It was about preventing a far greater disaster. The final confrontation was imminent, the stakes higher than ever before. The arrival in Philadelphia drew closer, a looming deadline on a desperate race against time.

The air hung thick with anticipation, a palpable tension that vibrated through the metal shell of the speeding train. Ava, huddled with her unlikely allies in the dimly lit restroom of the penultimate car, felt the weight of their audacious plan pressing down on her. Marco, his face pale and etched with exhaustion, meticulously traced a crude map of the train's interior onto a napkin, his shaky hand betraying the enormity of the risk they were about to undertake. Beside him, the former military medic, Sergeant Miller, meticulously checked his makeshift medical kit, his grim expression hinting at the grim reality of their situation. The tech-savvy student, Liam, hunched over his laptop, his fingers flying across the keyboard, hacking into the train's security system, a silent warrior in the digital battlefield. And finally, Mrs. Petrov, the elderly woman whose surprising strength had initially been dismissed, now sat quietly, her gaze resolute, a silent testament to her unwavering determination.

Their plan was a delicate tapestry woven from desperation and improvisation. They would exploit the train's layout, its inherent vulnerabilities, to their advantage. The baggage car, the most secure area, held the "package," a fact that had become their new primary objective. Getting there would require traversing the length of the train, navigating through cars filled with increasingly agitated hostages and Seraphina's heavily armed henchmen. Each car was a potential battlefield, each door a possible point of no return.

Liam's hacking efforts yielded a partial blueprint of the train's surveillance system. While Seraphina had secured the main cameras, several blind spots remained, small cracks in the seemingly impenetrable security. These were their escape routes, the subtle avenues they would use to navigate the labyrinthine corridors of the train unnoticed. The challenge, however, wasn't just stealth; it was also timing. They needed to strike precisely, minimizing the time spent in exposed areas while maximizing their chances of success.

"The dining car is our first obstacle," Miller stated, his voice low and measured. "Seraphina's men are heavily concentrated there. We'll need a distraction."

Mrs. Petrov, surprisingly, volunteered. "I shall create that distraction." Her calm tone belied a hidden steeliness, a quiet strength that resonated with an unexpected power. She had a plan, a simple yet effective strategy that involved utilizing the train's public address system, a feat Liam had managed to briefly unlock. She would broadcast a false alarm, diverting the attention of the guards long enough for the others to make their move.

Ava felt a tremor of apprehension. Their alliance was fragile, built on a foundation of shared danger and mutual distrust. One wrong move, one betrayal, and their carefully constructed plan would crumble, potentially leading to their demise. Yet, they had no choice but to trust each other, to rely on the skills and abilities of this unlikely team. Their survival, and potentially the safety of the entire train, depended on their combined strength, their seamless coordination.

The plan unfolded in a series of meticulously choreographed movements. Mrs. Petrov's false alarm, a cleverly worded announcement of a supposed gas leak, caused pandemonium in the dining car. The sudden rush of passengers towards the exits created an opportunity for Ava and her team to slip past the momentarily distracted guards. They moved with the precision of a well-oiled machine, a ballet of calculated risks and daring maneuvers.

The journey through the train was a tense, breathless affair. The darkness of the corridors, the rhythmic clatter of the train, the muffled cries of the hostages, all added to the ominous atmosphere. They encountered pockets of resistance, tense standoffs with Seraphina's men, moments where the fragile alliance felt threatened. But through it all, they persevered, driven by a shared sense of purpose and a growing desperation. They were not only fighting for their own lives but also for the potential prevention of a far greater catastrophe.

The baggage car proved to be the most challenging hurdle. It was heavily fortified, guarded by several of Seraphina's most trusted men. Liam's hacking efforts proved invaluable, allowing them to temporarily disable the car's internal security system, creating a short window of opportunity. The confrontation was swift and brutal, a short, sharp burst of action that tested their skills and courage to their limits. Marco, surprisingly resourceful, utilized his knowledge of the train's mechanics to overcome a crucial obstacle, demonstrating a surprising level of competence.

They located the package – a small, unmarked steel briefcase – hidden beneath a pile of luggage. Its contents remained a mystery, a tantalizing enigma that added to the tension of their desperate escape. As they secured the briefcase, the alarm blared, signaling that their window of opportunity was closing. They had to get off the baggage car, back to a place they could access the train's exit.

The escape was just as fraught with danger as the journey to the baggage car. Seraphina's men were alerted, their pursuit relentless. They battled their way through the train, the fight escalating in intensity with every passing moment. Ava found herself face to face with Seraphina herself, a chilling encounter that tested her resolve. The final confrontation was a chaotic clash of wills, a desperate struggle for survival amidst the claustrophobic confines of the speeding train.

As the train shuddered to a halt at Philadelphia station, Ava and her team emerged victorious, but battered and bruised. The package was secured, and Seraphina and her remaining cohorts were apprehended by the authorities, their reign of terror abruptly ended. The intricate plot, the shifting sands of alliances, the high-stakes confrontations, and the desperate measures – all culminated in a tense, breathless climax that left a lasting impression on both the characters and the readers. The beauty of the outside world was a stark contrast to the battle that took place within the train. Ava had not only avenged her family but had also prevented a disaster of potentially global proportions, a testament to her courage, resilience, and the unlikely alliances that had been forged in the crucible of danger. The aftermath, however, was far from certain, as the true nature of the package remained a mystery, leaving the door open for future events.

The dining car, bathed in the warm glow of artificial light, was a deceptive haven of chaos. Mrs. Petrov, a seemingly frail figure, stood before the train's public address system, her eyes blazing with a fierce determination that belied her age. With a steady hand, she activated the microphone, her voice, amplified through the train's speakers, cutting through the low murmur of conversation. "Attention passengers," she announced, her voice calm yet firm, tinged with a hint of manufactured panic. "We have a critical situation. A gas leak has been detected in the rear carriages. Please evacuate the area immediately and proceed to the nearest emergency exit."

The effect was immediate. A wave of panic rippled through the dining car. Passengers scrambled to their feet, pushing and shoving, a frantic tide of humanity surging towards the exits. The guards, initially bewildered, were quickly overwhelmed by the sudden surge of panicked passengers. This orchestrated chaos provided the perfect cover for Ava and her team. They moved like shadows, slipping through the gaps in the crowd, their movements fluid and precise. Marco, ever vigilant, kept a watchful eye on their surroundings, his hand resting on the makeshift weapon he'd fashioned from a broken bottle. Liam, his gaze fixed on the train's security monitors, subtly guided their movements, warning them of any approaching guards. Sergeant Miller, ever the pragmatist, maintained a rearguard position, ready to provide cover if necessary.

Their journey through the subsequent carriages was a relentless test of nerves and agility. Each car presented a unique challenge, a different obstacle to overcome. In one, they had to navigate a cramped corridor filled with sleeping passengers, their breaths held tight to avoid detection. In another, they faced a group of Seraphina's men playing cards, their casual demeanor masking a latent menace. A tense standoff ensued, a silent battle of wills, a delicate dance on the razor's edge of discovery. Marco, displaying an unexpected agility, disarmed one of the guards with a swift, precise movement, his normally mild demeanor replaced with a fierce determination. Liam's hacking skills allowed them to temporarily disable the security cameras in several areas, creating brief windows of opportunity. They moved with the synchronized precision of a well-trained military unit, their individual skills complementing each other perfectly. Ava, leading the charge, felt a growing sense of confidence, a surge of adrenaline fueling her determination.

The baggage car was a fortress, a steel-plated behemoth bristling with security measures. Thick steel doors, reinforced locks, and heavily armed guards guarded its entrance. Liam, working furiously on his laptop, managed to exploit a vulnerability in the train's network, creating a temporary blackout in the baggage car's surveillance system. This brief window of opportunity was all they needed. They launched their assault with the ferocity of a storm, their movements swift and decisive. The fight was brutal, a close-quarters melee fought in the cramped confines of the baggage car. The air filled with the clang of metal on metal, the grunts of exertion, and the sharp crack of breaking bones. Ava, demonstrating surprising strength and skill, engaged Seraphina's lead enforcer, a hulking brute who had underestimated her capabilities. The fight was fierce, a desperate struggle for dominance, but Ava, fueled by her burning desire for revenge, managed to subdue him.

The briefcase, small and unmarked, was hidden beneath a stack of oversized luggage. Its contents remained a mystery, an enigma that added to the tension of the situation. The weight of it felt heavy in Ava's hands, its metallic surface cold against her skin. The sense of accomplishment was fleeting, however. The alarm blared, signaling the end of their brief respite. The power was back on, and Seraphina's men were alerted. The escape was a desperate race against time, a frantic dash through the labyrinthine corridors of the train. They were hunted, pursued by a relentless pack of heavily armed criminals, their every move shadowed by the imminent threat of capture. The train, once a symbol of their meticulous plan, now felt like a suffocating cage, the very metal walls closing in on them.

The final confrontation took place in the almost deserted train carriage at the very end of the train. The pounding of the wheels against the tracks felt deafening in the ensuing silence as Ava and her team cornered

Seraphina and her remaining lieutenants. Seraphina, a ruthless woman with a cold gaze and a chilling demeanor, stood defiant, her face set in a grim expression. She was not merely a criminal; she was a master manipulator, a calculating strategist who had underestimated her opponents' resourcefulness. The fight that followed was a desperate clash of wills, a brutal dance of violence and adrenaline. Marco used his knowledge of the train's engineering to create diversions, while Liam fought with surprising skill and ferocity, employing his technical knowledge in unexpected ways. Sergeant Miller, ever practical, provided vital medical support while Ava and Seraphina faced off in a final, brutal showdown. Ava, despite her exhaustion, fought with a fierce determination, driven by years of pent-up anger and grief.

The fight spilled out into the corridor, ending with Ava holding Seraphina at gunpoint, her face contorted with a mixture of relief, exhaustion, and raw fury. Seraphina's defeat wasn't a clean victory; it was a brutal end to a relentless pursuit. Ava felt nothing but grim satisfaction. The train screeched to a halt at Philadelphia station, breaking the suffocating tension that had held the air captive during the journey. The arrival of the authorities ended the immediate danger, but the weight of their actions, the moral ambiguities of their choices, and the chilling uncertainty of the briefcase's contents remained.

Their survival had come at a cost, leaving a trail of emotional and physical scars. They emerged from the train, the relief palpable yet tinged with the sobering realization that their ordeal was far from over. The contents of the briefcase, the true nature of their mission, remained shrouded in mystery. The shifting sands of their alliance, the betrayals narrowly averted, and the chilling confrontation with Seraphina had all contributed to a harrowing experience that would forever shape their lives. The quiet hum of the station, a stark contrast to the chaos they had just escaped, couldn't fully mask the undercurrent of unease that lingered, a testament to the lingering questions that remained. The true cost of their victory was yet to be fully reckoned.

The train lurched, the screech of metal on metal a jarring counterpoint to the sudden silence that had fallen over Ava and her team. They stood amidst the wreckage of their battle with Seraphina and her men, the air thick with the metallic tang of blood and the acrid scent of burnt electronics. Ava, her breath ragged, leaned against the cold steel wall, her hand still trembling slightly from the adrenaline's lingering grip. The briefcase lay open on the floor beside her, its contents finally revealed. It wasn't the incriminating evidence they had expected; instead, it held a single, meticulously crafted flash drive.

Liam, his face pale but his eyes sharp, approached Ava, his movements cautious. "I've analyzed the data," he whispered, his voice low and strained. "It's...complicated." He hesitated, choosing his words carefully. "It's not evidence against Seraphina. It's something...else."

He held up the flash drive. "This contains a series of encrypted files. I've managed to decrypt some, but others... they're protected by a multi-layered encryption protocol I've never encountered before. It's military-grade."

Ava felt a cold dread creep into her heart. "What does it show?" she asked, her voice barely a breath. The relief she had felt moments before, the sense of closure, evaporated like morning mist. The victory felt hollow, the taste of success tainted by a growing unease.

Liam took a deep breath. "It shows...financial transactions. Massive amounts of money. Transferred to various offshore accounts. But the names... they're...familiar." He paused, his gaze locking with Ava's. "One of them is Sergeant Miller's."

The revelation hit Ava like a physical blow. Sergeant Miller, their steady hand, their pragmatic voice of reason, the man who had consistently maintained a cool head throughout the chaos, was implicated in a conspiracy far larger than they had ever imagined. The carefully constructed facade of their alliance crumbled, replaced by a chilling sense of betrayal. The trust, the camaraderie forged in the crucible of their shared struggle, shattered into a million pieces. She stared at Miller, his face impassive, his eyes revealing nothing. He remained silent, his expression unchanged.

Marco, ever observant, stepped forward. "What does it mean?" he asked, his voice laced with suspicion. "Is this a setup? A double-cross?"

Ava remained silent, her mind racing. The carefully crafted plan, the meticulous preparation, the risks they had taken – all of it could have been orchestrated by someone within their own ranks. The carefully laid foundation of their alliance was now stained with doubt and uncertainty. Trust, that essential element for their survival, had eroded. The train station was drawing closer, each second bringing them closer to the harsh reality of their predicament. They had defeated Seraphina, but a far more insidious enemy might be lurking among them.

The implications of Liam's discovery were devastating. Sergeant Miller, a seasoned police officer, seemed the least likely candidate for betrayal. Yet, the evidence was undeniable. The question gnawed at Ava, eating away at the fragile peace she had thought to have finally achieved: Could Sergeant Miller have been working with Seraphina all along? Was this a sophisticated double-cross, a carefully orchestrated plot to divert attention while someone else made their escape? Or was he a pawn in a larger game, unknowingly involved in a web of criminal activity he couldn't comprehend?

The approaching station loomed large in their minds, each rumble of the train's wheels serving as a stark reminder of the impending reckoning. Their carefully crafted plan, their hard-won victory, felt like ashes in their mouths, replaced by the bitter taste of suspicion and betrayal. The quiet hum of the approaching station did nothing to soothe their fraught nerves, as the revelation had shaken their already tenuous reality.

Ava forced herself to think clearly, her mind sifting through the events of the past few hours. Miller had always been cautious, his movements precise, his actions seemingly motivated by a single-minded focus on their goal. Had she missed something? Were there subtle hints she'd overlooked, signs of his treachery masked by his seemingly unwavering loyalty? She reviewed every interaction they had, searching for inconsistencies, looking for any clues she might have missed.

She studied Miller's face, his expression unchanged, his eyes still betraying nothing. He held her gaze steadily, never flinching. His silence was a deafening accusation, a cold confirmation of her suspicions. She saw a coldness in his eyes, a detached calmness, that spoke volumes.

"Miller," she said, her voice low, devoid of emotion. "Explain."

He didn't flinch. He didn't respond. His silence was a confirmation of his guilt, a silent admission of a betrayal that was far deeper than they ever could have anticipated.

The train screeched to a halt. The doors opened, revealing the bustling Philadelphia station. The arrival of the authorities had been anticipated, yet the relief was subdued, diluted by the harsh reality of Miller's betrayal. Outside the train, the world seemed to spin in a chaotic ballet. The arrival of the police created an immediate sense of unease as they surveyed the scene before them, observing the survivors and the carnage left behind. The weight of their predicament was tangible, suffocating.

The shifting sands of their alliance, the betrayals, the unexpected turns — all culminated in this moment of crisis, a crossroads where the lines between ally and enemy were blurred beyond recognition. The initial victory had been short-lived, replaced by a deeper and more treacherous conflict. The briefcase, once a symbol of their triumph, was now a testament to the intricacies of the deception that had ensnared them.

The train station, once a symbol of their intended destination, now represented the beginning of a new chapter, one that was far more perilous and uncertain than they had anticipated. They emerged into the chaotic environment of the station, the hustle and bustle of the crowds serving as a grim reminder of the unpredictability of their world. The journey, they realized, was far from over.

Ava's gaze locked with Miller's one last time before the police separated them, their silent exchange a final confirmation of the shattered trust. The truth, she knew, was still shrouded in layers of deception, its intricacies as complex as the intricate mechanisms of the train itself. The shifting sands beneath their feet threatened to bury them beneath the weight of betrayal and unresolved questions. The game had changed, and the stakes had been raised. Their battle for justice had morphed into a struggle for survival, a desperate fight against unseen forces, and against the ever-present threat of betrayal from within. As the sirens wailed in the distance, she knew that their journey had only just begun. The true reckoning was yet to come. The weight of their actions, the chilling uncertainty of Miller's motivations, and the lingering questions surrounding the flash drive's contents hung heavy in the air, a promise of more betrayals and revelations yet to come.

Chapter 3
The Chase

The train lurched violently, throwing Ava against Liam, who grunted in surprise. The rhythmic clatter of the wheels, previously a constant companion, was now punctuated by jarring metallic shrieks and the panicked shouts of passengers. Through a shattered window, Ava saw a blur of motion – a dark SUV, its headlights cutting through the pre-dawn gloom, paralleling the train's relentless speed. It was them, Seraphina's men, attempting a daring pursuit.

Marco, ever the pragmatist, was already assessing the situation. "They're trying to force a confrontation," he yelled over the rising din, his voice strained. "We need to make a move."

Ava gripped the edge of her seat, her gaze locked on the pursuing vehicle. The confined space of the train car, usually a source of claustrophobia, now felt like a cage, limiting their options, intensifying the pressure. Escape seemed impossible; the relentless pursuit made a clean getaway improbable. Their previous victory felt distant, a fading memory in the face of this renewed threat.

Liam, despite the chaos, was already working on a counter-strategy. "The next stop is Harrisburg," he shouted, his voice tight with urgency. "If we can make it to the next station, we can possibly lose them. But it's going to be a close call."

Their escape was fraught with peril. Each swaying movement of the train, each turn of the track, amplified the tension. Seraphina's men were relentless; the SUV's proximity felt menacing, a constant reminder of their imminent danger. Ava felt the adrenaline surge, a potent cocktail of fear and determination fueling her every action.

The train's interior was a battleground, a chaotic mixture of panicked passengers and desperate attempts at evasion. The initial struggle with Seraphina's men had left a trail of destruction – shattered glass, overturned seats, and the lingering scent of gunpowder. The air crackled with tension; every shadow held the potential for danger.

Ava, using her knowledge of the train's layout, guided her team through the maze of corridors and passenger cars, utilizing the narrow passages to their advantage. They were a whirlwind of calculated movements, their actions born of desperate necessity and years of training. The rhythmic clatter of the wheels, the swaying motion of the train, became their rhythm, the soundtrack of their daring escape.

Their unlikely alliance, forged in the fires of their shared ordeal, was tested by this desperate chase. Miller, despite the shadow of suspicion hanging over him, played a crucial role, his years of experience evident in his calm, precise movements. He provided invaluable insights, his understanding of law enforcement procedures invaluable in navigating the train's corridors, staying one step ahead of their relentless pursuers.

The confrontation between Ava and Miller, however, remained unspoken. The accusation hung heavy between them, an invisible wall separating their physical proximity. Her gaze constantly drifted towards him, observing his every move, her mind replaying every interaction, searching for subtle cues, inconsistencies, any evidence that would corroborate or refute her suspicions.

The next stop, Harrisburg, drew nearer, each passing moment feeling like an eternity. The train seemed to crawl, the SUV relentlessly close on their trail. Ava could almost feel the heat of its headlights through the shattered glass, a burning reminder of the immediate danger.

As the train approached Harrisburg, a daring plan took shape. Ava devised a strategy that involved separating from the main group, creating a diversion. Marco would create a distraction in the opposite direction, drawing Seraphina's attention away from Ava and Miller. This bold maneuver, filled with inherent risk, could offer them a sliver of opportunity.

The Harrisburg station loomed, its lights a beacon of potential salvation or catastrophic failure. The train's screech was a deafening announcement of their approach, the sounds blending with the roar of the engine and the relentless pursuit from behind. Time was running out.

The execution of their plan was seamless, a ballet of controlled chaos. Marco, with his usual flair for theatrics, triggered a minor disruption, creating confusion and diversion amongst the other passengers. His act was convincing, drawing the attention of Seraphina's men away from Ava and Miller.

Ava and Miller, however, utilized a different route, slipping through a rarely used service corridor. They navigated the labyrinthine passages beneath the train, the air thick with the smell of oil and coal dust. The journey was treacherous, their movements careful, guided by Miller's knowledge of the train's underbelly.

Their escape became a race against time, a silent negotiation with fate. The rhythmic beat of the train, the distant sound of the pursuing vehicle, punctuated by the steady thud of their footsteps. The tension, however, was palpable, laced with desperation, and the constant threat of discovery.

They reached their destination, a small, unassuming side exit, a rarely used passage concealed in the shadows, long before the pursuing SUV could intercept them. They emerged from the dark, damp underbelly of the train into the night, the fresh air a stark contrast to the claustrophobic confines they had just escaped.

They were safe, for now. The escape was a hard-won victory, a testament to their resilience and their ability to adapt, to improvise, and to trust their instincts. The shadow of Miller's betrayal, however, remained, an unspoken truth that cast a pall over their success. They had escaped Seraphina, but the true reckoning, the confrontation between Ava and Miller, loomed large, yet to be reckoned with. The game was far from over. The escape, though successful, felt like a mere reprieve, a temporary respite before the storm broke. The next act, the pursuit of justice and the unraveling of the truth, lay before them. Harrisburg was merely a waypoint on a journey that was far from over. The true battle, the pursuit of justice and the ultimate reckoning, lay ahead. The weight of unanswered questions, the lingering suspicion, and the looming confrontation with Miller created an ominous undercurrent, a palpable tension that threatened to unravel their fragile alliance. The chase was over, but the game, they both knew, had just begun.

The train lurched again, this time more violently, throwing Ava against the cold metal of the emergency exit. The jarring impact knocked the wind out of her, and for a moment, everything went black around the edges. She gasped, clutching her side, the pain sharp and insistent. The SUV, still hot on their trail, was gaining. The rhythmic pounding of its engine, a relentless predator closing in for the kill, was almost audible even above the train's deafening roar.

Liam, ever the strategist, was already barking orders, his face grim. "Tunnel ahead!" he yelled, his voice barely audible above the din. "Get down! They won't be able to see us." The sudden darkness, as the train plunged into the inky blackness of the tunnel, was a welcome shroud, a temporary reprieve from the relentless glare of the pursuing headlights.

The darkness was absolute, a thick, suffocating blanket that swallowed the train whole. The rhythmic clatter of the wheels was muted, replaced by an eerie silence broken only by the occasional groan of the metal under stress and the frantic whispers of the passengers. Ava felt a surge of claustrophobia, the enclosed space of the train car pressing in on her, amplifying her already heightened anxiety. The air, thick with the smell of coal dust and fear, seemed to weigh down her lungs.

Miller, despite his usual stoicism, seemed visibly shaken. The close call had clearly rattled him, the usual calm precision in his movements replaced with a nervous energy. He kept glancing over his shoulder, his eyes darting nervously in the darkness, betraying his unease. The accusation still hung heavy in the air between him and Ava, a silent tension that crackled in the darkness.

Marco, surprisingly, was the calmest of the group. He moved with a practiced efficiency, checking on the passengers, calming their fears with a practiced ease that bordered on the theatrical. His usual bravado, however, was laced with a palpable tension. He knew, as they all did, that the tunnel was a double-edged sword. It offered temporary respite from their pursuers, but it also trapped them in a confined, vulnerable space.

The darkness, however, was not their only enemy. The tunnel itself was fraught with danger. The train's speed, previously a source of escape, now felt like a threat. A sudden jolt, a screech of metal, and the train lurched violently, throwing the already tense passengers into a state of near-panic. Ava braced herself, fearing the worst.

The darkness amplified every sound, every creak and groan of the train, each echoing in the claustrophobic space, turning every shadow into a potential threat. Ava could feel her heart pounding in her chest, a frantic drumbeat against the silence. She held her breath, her senses heightened, listening, waiting for the next unexpected jolt, the next potential disaster.

As the train continued its terrifying journey through the darkness, the situation escalated. One of the train's lights flickered and died, plunging a section of the car into complete darkness. A collective gasp rippled through the passengers. The ensuing chaos provided an opening for one of Seraphina's men, who had managed to infiltrate the train during the initial attack.

The man, a hulking figure silhouetted against the faint light from the remaining lamps, lunged forward, aiming a silenced pistol at Miller. Before the man could pull the trigger, however, Liam reacted with surprising speed, tackling the attacker to the floor. A fierce struggle ensued, a brutal ballet of grappling limbs and muffled grunts in the darkness.

Ava, her adrenaline surging, acted on instinct. She grabbed a nearby fire extinguisher, and with a powerful swing, brought it crashing down on the attacker's head. The man crumpled, unconscious. The sudden and unexpected act was met with shocked silence from the passengers. The tension in the air was almost palpable, the darkness suddenly heavy with the weight of near-death and unspoken fear.

The incident served to strengthen their fragile alliance. The shared brush with death had forged an unspoken bond, a camaraderie born from shared peril. The lines between victim and perpetrator blurred, as their fight for survival overshadowed their individual goals and prejudices.

The tunnel seemed to stretch on forever, the darkness an oppressive presence. The sounds of the train—the rhythmic clatter of the wheels, the rumble of the engine, the occasional groan of the metal—were punctuated by the ragged breathing of the passengers and the rhythmic thump-thump-thump of Ava's own heart.

As they finally emerged from the tunnel, blinking in the sudden brightness of the dawn, they were met with a breathtaking sight. The sunrise, painting the sky in shades of orange and pink, offered a moment of fragile beauty, a stark contrast to the darkness they had just escaped. The beauty, however, was fleeting, the relief temporary. The SUV was still visible in the distance, a persistent shadow, a reminder of their precarious situation. The chase was far from over. The escape from the tunnel, harrowing as it was, was merely another chapter in their fight for survival, another step in their desperate journey towards justice. The game was still afoot, the stakes higher than ever. The fragile alliance forged in the heart of the darkness, however, had been strengthened, forged anew in the crucible of shared terror and near-death. The road ahead, however, remained uncertain, the shadows lurking, the path treacherous.

The jarring sunlight, a stark contrast to the suffocating darkness of the tunnel, momentarily blinded Ava. She shielded her eyes, the adrenaline still coursing through her veins, a potent cocktail of fear and exhilaration. The SUV, a relentless predator, was still in pursuit, its headlights cutting through the morning mist like predatory eyes. Liam, his face grim, was already assessing their situation.

"They're gaining," he muttered, his voice tight with tension. "We need to act fast."

Miller, his composure restored, but his eyes betraying a lingering unease, checked the rear cars. Marco, his usual theatrical charm muted, was calmly assessing the situation, his eyes scanning the landscape for any possible escape routes. The passengers, a shaken and silent mass, huddled together, their faces a mixture of fear and exhaustion.

Suddenly, Marco stopped, his hand flying to his earpiece. His expression shifted, from one of grim determination to stunned disbelief. He turned to Ava, his voice barely a whisper, "They... they're using a different line. A freight line. This... this isn't an accident."

Ava felt a chill crawl down her spine. The precision of the pursuit, the seemingly random acts of violence, the sudden change in tactics – it all pointed to something more orchestrated, more sinister. It wasn't just a random act of crime; it was a calculated maneuver, part of a larger, more elaborate plan.

Liam, ever the pragmatist, immediately began barking orders, his voice sharp and decisive. "We need to get off this train. Now."

But where? And how? The train was hurtling towards Philadelphia, each passing moment bringing them closer to the criminals' intended destination, closer to the inevitable confrontation. The landscape whizzed by, a blur of green fields and distant farmhouses. Escape seemed impossible. The freight line was unexpected, a strategic move the criminals hadn't anticipated. But the unexpected move also threw their calculations off.

Then, amidst the chaos, a small detail caught Ava's eye. A discarded briefcase, lying half-hidden beneath a seat, near where Seraphina's man had attacked Miller. It was a simple, unassuming briefcase, nothing extraordinary in appearance, but instinct told her it held a key piece of the puzzle.

Cautiously, Ava approached, her hand hovering over the clasp. The leather felt strangely smooth, almost new, in stark contrast to the worn upholstery of the train seats. She carefully opened it, her breath catching in her throat as she saw its contents: a meticulously organized set of files, detailing not only the financial transactions of Seraphina's syndicate, but also a network of corporate connections and coded messages. But the most startling discovery was a photograph – a picture of Miller, younger, smiling, with a woman who bore an uncanny resemblance to Seraphina.

The blood drained from Ava's face. The revelation hit her with the force of a physical blow. Miller wasn't just an unwitting victim. He was connected to Seraphina, deeply involved in her web of deceit. He had been playing a double game, feigning innocence while secretly aiding in Seraphina's escape and the execution of her plan. The shock of the betrayal was almost unbearable.

The implications were staggering. Miller's actions explained the precise timing of the train hijacking, the seemingly random attacks, and his reluctance to directly engage with Seraphina's men. He'd been carefully orchestrating their escape. The betrayal stung, a bitter taste in her mouth, eroding the fragile trust they had built during the harrowing journey through the tunnel.

Liam, noticing Ava's stricken expression and the file in her hand, looked at her in silent question. He was quick to understand the gravity of the revelation, his face etched with a mixture of anger, confusion, and something else – a dawning realization of their perilous situation. The man they had trusted, their potential ally, was the key to the whole scheme. The enemy was among them.

Marco, ever the pragmatist, moved swiftly. He quickly scanned the files, his fingers flying across the documents, confirming Ava's discovery. His expression was grim. He confirmed the connection between Miller and Seraphina, and added another layer of complexity to the already chaotic situation. Miller's betrayal had not only jeopardized their mission, it could cost them their lives. The stakes had just been raised exponentially.

"We can't trust him," Marco stated simply, his tone devoid of emotion. "He's playing both sides. We need to act quickly, and we need to act decisively."

Time was running out. Philadelphia was drawing nearer, its skyline already visible on the horizon. The train was slowing, approaching the station, the end of the line. They needed a plan, and they needed it now.

The situation was now far more complex than a simple revenge mission. It was a battle for survival against a cunning adversary who knew their every move, a betrayal that shattered their fragile alliance, and a race against time to expose the truth and bring those responsible to justice before they escaped.

With Miller revealed as a double-agent, the situation shifted into a new level of uncertainty and danger. The carefully constructed alliances crumbled, leaving Ava and her remaining allies with no option but to fight for survival amidst the escalating chaos. The train was becoming a death trap. The train was a cage.

Ava, her heart pounding a relentless rhythm against her ribs, felt a surge of cold determination. Betrayal sharpened her senses, fueling her resolve. She would not let Miller's treachery derail her mission. She would not let her family's memory be dishonored by a cowardly escape.

She looked at Liam and Marco, their faces mirrored her own determination. The fragile alliance forged in the darkness of the tunnel had been shattered, but a new, colder resolve had taken its place. This wasn't just about revenge anymore; it was about survival.

The train slowed to a halt, the screech of brakes cutting through the morning air. Philadelphia loomed before them, its imposing buildings a stark contrast to the confined and claustrophobic space of the speeding train. The arrival at the station brought a mix of dread and desperate hope. The criminals' carefully laid plan was about to reach its end-game. The tension was palpable, thick enough to taste. The air crackled with the impending confrontation. They would stop the criminals. They would expose the truth. No matter the cost. The battle for justice was about to begin. The final act would play out in the heart of the city.

The passengers, still shaken and disoriented, remained silent as the train doors opened. The platform teemed with activity; a scene of controlled chaos that mirrored the turmoil brewing within the train. The escape was far from secured; Philadelphia presented its own challenges, its network of hidden routes, a maze to navigate. But Ava knew they had to act quickly, every second counting as the criminals sought to disappear into the city. The city, a potential prison and a potential path to freedom, held their future in its uncertain embrace.

The city's vastness was a double-edged sword, offering both a sanctuary and a labyrinth of potential dangers. They had to find a way to expose Miller, to stop Seraphina and her network, and bring them to justice. The challenge was immense, the odds stacked against them. Yet, fueled by the burning desire for justice and the cold fury of betrayal, Ava, Liam, and Marco were ready. The game had changed, the stakes had been raised, and the final act was about to begin. The chase was far from over, but it was about to enter its most dangerous and decisive phase. The fight for justice would be a bloody one. The fight for survival, even more so. Philadelphia waited.

The dining car, usually a picture of elegant calm, was now a battlefield. Crystal glasses lay shattered on the plush carpets, mingling with the crimson stain spreading across the pristine white tablecloth. The air, thick with the scent of expensive wine and the metallic tang of blood, vibrated with a tension so palpable it felt like a physical presence.

Ava, her face streaked with grime and blood, stood over Miller, his body slumped against the mahogany paneling, a single, fatal bullet wound marring his perfectly tailored suit. Liam, his usually calm demeanor replaced by a controlled fury, held his weapon, the barrel still smoking. Marco, his face grim, stood guard, his eyes scanning the room for any sign of further trouble. The opulent setting formed a stark contrast to the brutality that had unfolded, the juxtaposition highlighting the grotesque nature of the violence.

The confrontation had been swift, brutal, and necessary. Miller, his betrayal exposed, had attempted to escape, using his knowledge of the train's layout and his familiarity with Seraphina's men to gain an advantage. He had tried to silence them, to eliminate the witnesses to his treachery. But Ava and her allies had been faster, more ruthless.

The revelation of Miller's double life had unleashed a torrent of raw emotion. Liam, grappling with the weight of his own past betrayals, had reacted with visceral rage, the years of pent-up anger and frustration exploding in a single, decisive act. Ava, her carefully constructed plans shattered, felt a cold fury unlike anything she had ever known. The betrayal was a fresh wound, tearing open old scars.

As the adrenaline subsided, a wave of exhaustion washed over them, leaving behind a chilling emptiness. The fight had been won, but at a steep cost. The silence in the aftermath was deafening, broken only by the rhythmic clatter of the train's wheels against the tracks. The weight of their actions, the moral complexities of their choices, pressed down on them, a heavy burden they would carry long after the dust settled.

Marco, ever the pragmatist, broke the silence. "We need to assess the situation," he said, his voice low and steady. "Seraphina's men are still out there. We can't let our guard down."

He moved to examine the bodies, his movements precise and efficient. He confirmed Miller's death, then moved on to check the other casualties. The carnage was extensive, a stark reminder of the brutal fight that had just ended.

Ava, her gaze fixed on Miller's lifeless form, allowed herself a brief moment of reflection. She had killed a man. A man she had once considered an ally. A man who was, in many ways, a victim of Seraphina's manipulative web. The moral ambiguity was a heavy burden to bear, a constant reminder of the grey areas that existed in this deadly game of revenge. Justice was a double-edged sword, its sharp blade capable of inflicting as much pain as it promised to heal.

The discovery of Miller's past, unearthed amidst the chaos of the confrontation, further complicated the picture. He had been a victim of Seraphina's network himself, manipulated and exploited, his own emotional trauma used as a weapon against him. His involvement with Seraphina had been born out of desperation, a desperate attempt to escape his past, to find redemption in a world that had offered him none.

His story was a grim reminder of the insidious nature of Seraphina's operation, its ability to manipulate and corrupt even those who appeared to be immune. His past, a tangled web of broken promises and shattered dreams, served as a chilling illustration of the far-reaching consequences of Seraphina's manipulation, painting a grim portrait of her enduring influence, long after her physical presence had departed.

The weight of these revelations bore heavily upon Ava. She had sought revenge, but in doing so, she had become entangled in a web of complex morality, finding herself forced to make agonizing choices that challenged her very sense of justice. She had sought to right a wrong, but in doing so, she had created new ones, leaving her to grapple with the bitter taste of unintended consequences.

Liam, his composure gradually returning, moved to collect the evidence. The scattered files, the shattered glasses, the blood-soaked carpet – all fragments of a puzzle that needed to be pieced together before the train reached Philadelphia. Each piece, no matter how seemingly insignificant, would aid in understanding the broader reach of Seraphina's operation.

He gathered the relevant files, carefully preserving any clues that might lead to Seraphina's capture. He examined Miller's possessions, searching for any further evidence that might provide answers to the lingering questions. His methodical approach was a stark contrast to the chaos that had just engulfed the dining car, providing a sense of order amidst the continuing uncertainty.

The train continued its relentless journey toward Philadelphia, each passing moment bringing them closer to their final confrontation with Seraphina. The city, now clearly visible on the horizon, represented both the culmination of their journey and the beginning of a new, even more treacherous phase in their pursuit of justice. The atmosphere in the train was heavy with anticipation, the silence punctuated only by the rhythmic chugging of the engine, each beat ticking closer towards the impending climax.

The revelation of Miller's past added yet another layer of complexity to the situation, blurring the lines between victim and perpetrator, between justice and revenge. Ava, Liam, and Marco, weary but determined, were left to wrestle with the moral complexities of their actions, the weight of their choices pressing heavily upon them as they approached the culmination of their long and dangerous journey.

Philadelphia, once a beacon of hope, now felt like a trap, a city of shadows where justice could be elusive and the pursuit of truth could lead to even greater peril. The city's sprawling network of streets and alleyways promised both escape and danger, a labyrinthine landscape where they would be forced to confront their past, their present, and their uncertain future. The journey was far from over. The final act was about to begin.

The rhythmic clatter of the train wheels against the tracks provided a monotonous soundtrack to their mounting unease. Philadelphia loomed on the horizon, a concrete monolith promising both resolution and further peril. The air hung heavy with the unspoken tension, the silence broken only by the occasional stifled cough or the nervous shuffling of feet. Ava, Liam, and Marco, each grappling with their own demons, moved through the ravaged dining car, the scene of their brutal encounter with Miller still etched into their minds.

Liam, meticulous as ever, continued his investigation. He meticulously documented the scene, photographing the scattered documents, the shattered glass, the bloodstains – each detail a potential piece of the puzzle leading to Seraphina. He carefully collected Miller's personal effects, searching for any clues that might shed light on his past, on his connection to Seraphina's organization, on the depth of her insidious reach. His sharp eyes, usually so calm, darted around, his mind racing, piecing together fragments of information, searching for a pattern, a connection that might lead them to Seraphina.

Marco, his pragmatic nature ever present, assessed the train's security. He moved silently through the carriages, checking doors, windows, and any potential escape routes for Seraphina's remaining henchmen. His experience in counter-terrorism operations made him acutely aware of the potential threats, his senses honed to perceive danger before it materialized. He communicated his observations to Ava and Liam in hushed whispers, his low voice a stark contrast to the escalating tension within the train.

Ava, meanwhile, found herself wrestling with the moral complexities of their actions. The death of Miller weighed heavily on her conscience, a stark reminder of the grey areas in her quest for revenge. She had sought justice, but had she become a perpetrator in her own right? The question gnawed at her, a relentless torment that threatened to consume her. She looked out of the window, the city of Philadelphia slowly growing larger, a looming presence that both terrified and galvanized her.

Suddenly, a piercing shriek shattered the oppressive silence. It originated from one of the passenger compartments, echoing through the train, raising their adrenaline levels instantly. They exchanged apprehensive glances, a silent acknowledgment of the potential threat. With practiced efficiency, they moved towards the source of the sound, their weapons ready. Liam took the lead, his years of military training equipping him with the necessary instinct and tactical prowess.

They found a young woman, cowering in a corner, her face pale, eyes wide with terror. She was clutching a small, battered radio, its antenna broken. She explained, in broken, panicked whispers, that she was a communications specialist, working freelance for various organizations. She had been a passenger on the train, a completely unrelated witness to the unfolding events. She had stumbled upon Seraphina's encrypted communications, intercepting crucial pieces of information regarding Seraphina's escape plan, her final destination, and her immediate plans for the hostages.

This was a stroke of unexpected luck, a turning point in their struggle. The young woman, whose name was Elara, possessed a unique skill set that could prove invaluable in their fight against Seraphina. Her ability to decode encrypted signals and her knowledge of communications technology gave them a critical edge. This chance encounter was a beacon of hope in the deepening shadows of their precarious situation.

Elara, despite her obvious terror, exhibited a surprising resilience and competence. She quickly explained the technical aspects of Seraphina's communication system, outlining their weaknesses and revealing the specifics of Seraphina's escape plan. She had managed to decipher parts of their communications before the hijacking, and now, with access to their equipment and her own portable tech, she could potentially disrupt Seraphina's plan to escape undetected. She could also provide real-time tracking and location data, significantly altering the parameters of their desperate gamble.

The team worked quickly, utilizing Elara's expertise to turn the tables. They used her knowledge to jam Seraphina's communication network, disrupting her ability to coordinate her actions and her escape route. Elara's technical prowess provided crucial insights into Seraphina's plans, allowing Liam, Marco, and Ava to anticipate her moves and formulate a counter-strategy. They were no longer simply fighting for survival; they were actively taking the initiative.

The train was hurtling towards Philadelphia, the city approaching like a looming threat. Time was running out. With Elara's help, they used the radio to transmit a distress signal to the authorities, a desperate attempt to alert them to the hijacking and Seraphina's impending escape. They knew the odds were slim, but it was a chance worth taking. They used her technical expertise to pinpoint Seraphina's location within the train and laid out a carefully coordinated plan to confront her.

As the train entered the outskirts of Philadelphia, the tension reached a fever pitch. Seraphina, realizing her communication network was compromised, reacted with her characteristic ruthlessness. She ordered her remaining men to secure the hostages, preparing for a final showdown, her escape route compromised, her patience exhausted. She needed to act quickly and decisively, her grasp on the situation slipping away. She had underestimated her adversaries, her confidence shaken by the unexpected appearance of Elara.

The final confrontation was unavoidable. The train pulled into Philadelphia Station. The passengers were terrified. The showdown had arrived. Ava, Liam, Marco, and their unlikely ally, Elara, were ready to confront Seraphina. The battle for justice, for survival, would now take place within the chaos and confines of Philadelphia's bustling railway station, amongst oblivious commuters. The weight of their actions, the culmination of their relentless pursuit, now hinged on the outcome of this final, desperate confrontation. The train screeched to a halt, signaling the beginning of the end. The city outside the windows was a vibrant, bustling metropolis – a stark contrast to the battleground within the train. The final act was about to begin.

Chapter 4
Philadelphia

The screech of brakes announced their arrival in Philadelphia, a jarring sound that sliced through the suffocating tension. The train shuddered to a halt, the sudden stillness amplifying the frantic beating of their hearts. Outside, the city throbbed with life, a stark contrast to the claustrophobic chaos within the carriages. The sounds of bustling commuters, the distant sirens, the cacophony of urban life, only served to heighten the sense of urgency. Their escape, once a carefully orchestrated plan, now felt like a desperate gamble.

Ava, her face grim, surveyed their surroundings. The station was a labyrinth of platforms, tunnels, and echoing hallways, a perfect hiding place for Seraphina and her remaining accomplices. The throngs of people, oblivious to the turmoil within the train, presented both a challenge and an opportunity – a sea of faces to blend into, a cover for their escape.

Liam, ever the strategist, quickly assessed the situation. He pointed out several potential escape routes, each fraught with peril. The main concourse, teeming with people, offered the best chance of anonymity, but it also increased the risk of detection. The less-trafficked service tunnels were a riskier option, offering concealment but a greater chance of being cornered. The decision rested on a precarious balance between speed and discretion.

Marco, his eyes scanning the platform, identified several potential obstacles: uniformed police officers patrolling the area, security cameras positioned at strategic points, and the ever-present threat of Seraphina's men lurking in the shadows. His experience in covert operations honed his perception, his mind a whirlwind of contingencies and potential risks. He quickly devised a plan to neutralize these threats.

Elara, her pale face reflecting the flickering lights of the station, worked tirelessly on her laptop. She was transmitting a heavily encrypted message to a contact in the National Security Agency, detailing the hijacking and Seraphina's escape plan. Despite her fear, she demonstrated unwavering professionalism, her fingers flying across the keyboard, navigating the complexities of digital security protocols. Her efforts were a last-ditch attempt to alert the authorities to their predicament and provide crucial information for the police investigation.

The decision was made. They would use the main concourse for their initial escape, relying on the chaos of the station to shield their movements. The risk was high, but the alternative – venturing into the claustrophobic service tunnels – was even more precarious. Liam and Marco would create a diversion, drawing attention away from Ava and Elara, giving them the opportunity to slip away unnoticed.

As the doors hissed open, Liam and Marco unleashed a coordinated assault. They burst out, firing several bursts of non-lethal rounds into the air, creating a scene of controlled chaos. Shrieks and shouts erupted from the bewildered passengers, a symphony of panic that masked their escape. The two men, moving with practiced precision, utilized their tactical skills, using the confusion to their advantage. They engaged the remaining henchmen, exchanging gunfire that sent passengers scattering for cover.

Ava and Elara, meanwhile, slipped out unnoticed, melting into the sea of commuters. Their objective: to reach the nearest exit, secure a vehicle, and reach their pre-arranged rendezvous point outside the city. The weight of their actions pressed down on them, the city's relentless pulse a deafening backdrop to their silent dash.

The chase was relentless. Seraphina, infuriated by their defiance, unleashed a relentless pursuit. Her men, fueled by adrenaline and desperation, relentlessly pursued Ava and Elara through the labyrinthine station. The pursuit was a frantic ballet of evasion, a desperate struggle for survival in the heart of a bustling city.

Ava, her adrenaline surging, navigated the throngs of people, her senses sharpened by the adrenaline coursing through her veins. Elara, despite her terror, remained surprisingly calm, her knowledge of the station's layout helping them evade their pursuers. They weaved through the crowds, their movements fluid and precise, a testament to their resourcefulness and determination.

The situation escalated when they stumbled upon a group of undercover police officers who were alerted to the incident by Elara's earlier transmission. A brief but intense firefight ensued, with Ava using her enhanced combat skills to protect Elara. The encounter was short-lived, with the police officers providing cover for their escape.

Despite the near-miss, they were far from safe. Seraphina's men continued the pursuit, their determination unyielding. Ava knew they needed to shake off their pursuers quickly. They were forced into a nearby alley, their escape routes blocked. It was here, in a dark, grimy alleyway, a world away from the polished glamour of the train, that the final confrontation was set to begin.

Seraphina emerged from the shadows, her face a mask of icy determination. Her eyes, cold and calculating, fixed on Ava, signaling a final, brutal showdown. The city's ambient noise faded as the sounds of combat filled the air. The echoes of gunfire, the metallic clang of steel, and the grunts of exertion formed a deadly counterpoint to the distant city hum. The fight was not just for survival; it was a clash of wills, a desperate struggle to reclaim a life shattered by betrayal and loss.

The battle was fierce and unrelenting. Ava, fueled by rage and a desperate need for justice, fought with the fury of a cornered animal. Elara, though unarmed, provided vital support, using her quick wits to distract Seraphina's men, buying Ava precious time. The fight was brutal, a chaotic ballet of strikes and blocks, of desperation and courage. The outcome hung in the balance, a knife's edge between victory and defeat.

The clash reached a climax amidst the gritty urban landscape. The sounds of the fight were swallowed by the city, yet the intensity remained palpable. The air hung heavy with the smell of gunpowder, sweat, and fear. In the heart of Philadelphia, amidst the chaos, the battle for justice would be determined. The city, a silent observer, stood as witness to the culmination of a meticulously planned revenge and a desperate struggle for survival. The outcome remained uncertain, a testament to the intricate web of betrayal and the blurred line between victim and perpetrator. The fate of Ava, Elara, and the city itself, hung precariously in the balance. The final act of this deadly game of cat and mouse was about to unfold.

The alley was a claustrophobic tomb, the brick walls closing in, damp and smelling of decay. The only light came from a flickering neon sign casting a sickly yellow glow on the grimy pavement. Ava, her breath ragged, leaned against the wall, the metallic tang of blood filling her mouth. Elara, her face ashen, huddled behind a overflowing dumpster, her eyes wide with terror. They had cornered them, but the advantage was fleeting. Seraphina's remaining men, three hardened criminals, circled them, their weapons drawn.

Seraphina herself stood a few feet away, her silhouette sharp against the neon light. She was composed, almost serene, despite the chaos swirling around her. The calculated precision of her movements belied the lethal intent in her eyes. She'd lost some of her men, but she wasn't deterred. This was personal. This was about retribution for the life she'd lost.

"You made a mistake, Ava," Seraphina hissed, her voice a low growl that cut through the night's stillness. "You thought you could escape? You thought you could take me down? You were wrong."

Ava spat blood onto the ground, her defiance undeterred. "This isn't over, Seraphina. You'll pay for what you did."

The ensuing fight was a brutal ballet of violence. Ava, fueled by adrenaline and a burning need for vengeance, moved with a savage grace. She was a whirlwind of motion, her movements precise and deadly. Each strike was calculated, each block a testament to her years of training. Liam's combat lessons echoed in her mind, shaping her every move, guiding her through the chaos. She weaved between Seraphina's men, dodging blows and landing devastating counterattacks.

Elara, despite her fear, played a crucial role. Her quick wit and knowledge of her surroundings proved invaluable. She threw a heavy metal pipe from the dumpster, striking one of Seraphina's men in the leg. The man screamed, collapsing to the ground, groaning in pain. This bought Ava precious seconds, allowing her to gain the upper hand. She moved like a phantom, taking down the others one by one, using the environment to her advantage – a swift kick to the chest, sending one sprawling; a quick swipe of a shard of broken glass, disabling another.

But Seraphina was relentless, a formidable opponent. She fought with the cold efficiency of a predator, her movements economical, each blow precise and powerful. Ava parried her attacks, but the fight was draining her. She felt the burn in her muscles, the sting of a deep gash on her arm, but her resolve remained unshaken. It was more than just a fight for survival; it was a fight for justice, for the memory of her family.

The fight spilled out onto the street. The sudden outburst of violence attracted attention. The alley, once a silent, forgotten corner of the city, was now a stage for a desperate battle. Sirens wailed in the distance, growing closer. Ava knew they didn't have much time.

In a moment of brutal hand-to-hand combat, Ava disarmed one of Seraphina's men, using his own weapon against him. She forced Seraphina into a corner, their fight blurring into a desperate exchange of blows. Ava aimed her weapon at Seraphina's head, but hesitated. The weight of the decision pressed down on her – the line between justice and revenge blurred. Seraphina had committed heinous crimes, but Ava was not without her own moral ambiguities. Her plan had morphed into something far more brutal and chaotic than she had intended. The echoes of the train, the screams of the hostages, the weight of the dead, pressed down on her.

Just as Ava was about to pull the trigger, a gunshot echoed in the air. One of Seraphina's men, regaining his footing, took a shot at Ava. Seraphina lunged forward, pushing Ava out of the way. The bullet grazed her shoulder, a searing pain ripping through her flesh. Ava reacted instantly, seizing the moment to disarm her final assailant. Seraphina crumpled to the ground, her eyes fixed on Ava, a mixture of disbelief and defeat etched on her face.

Police cars screeched to a halt, bathing the alley in flashing lights. Officers swarmed the scene, their weapons pointed, their eyes scanning the alley. Ava, panting, leaned against the wall, her body trembling with exhaustion, the taste of blood thick in her mouth. Elara rushed to her side, her eyes filled with concern.

The aftermath was a whirlwind of chaos. Ambulances arrived, sirens wailing, adding to the already cacophonous sounds of the city. The wounded were taken away, their cries muffled by the surrounding noise. The city, once a distant hum, was now a throbbing pulse of sirens, shouts, and flashing lights, a stark reminder of the night's violence.

Ava, hands raised, surrendered to the police. Despite the overwhelming sense of exhaustion, a feeling of relief washed over her. Justice, however flawed and brutal, had been served. The fight was over, but the long process of healing, both physical and emotional, had just begun. The events on the train to Philadelphia had irrevocably changed her. The city lights reflected in her weary eyes, mirroring the turmoil within her soul. The city itself had been a silent witness to the final showdown, to the culmination of a meticulously planned revenge, and to the fragile victory that had been won at a steep price. The echoes of gunfire and the distant wail of sirens remained, a grim reminder of the night's events, and the moral complexities that lay hidden beneath the surface of her victory. The train, the alley, the city – all of them bore witness to the grim price of revenge, a testament to the intricate dance between victim and perpetrator, and the blurred lines that separated them. The journey was far from over, but in the heart of Philadelphia, a chapter had closed.

The train lurched violently, throwing Ava against the cold metal of the wall. The hijacking had plunged the carriage into chaos; screams mingled with the clatter of gunfire and the desperate shouts of passengers. The meticulously planned revenge, the calculated precision of her actions, had all crumbled, leaving her in a desperate fight for survival. She'd managed to slip away from the initial onslaught, hiding amongst the terrified passengers, her heart hammering against her ribs. But Seraphina's men were relentless, their search methodical and brutal.

Liam, his face pale but determined, had helped her find a relatively secluded compartment. He'd been an unexpected ally, a corporate lawyer whose calm demeanor masked a surprising resilience. He had proven invaluable, his knowledge of the train's layout and his quick thinking saving them from several close calls. Elara, still shaken from the initial attack, was tending to a young boy, his arm bleeding profusely. Her gentle hands moved with practiced efficiency, applying pressure to the wound and whispering reassurances.

The air hung thick with fear, the metallic tang of blood and the acrid smell of gunpowder permeating the enclosed space. The rhythmic thumping of the train wheels on the tracks provided a stark counterpoint to the chaos within. Each jolt felt like a death knell, a reminder of their precarious situation. Ava knew they were running out of time. Seraphina, ruthless and efficient, would find them.

Suddenly, a deafening explosion rocked the train, throwing them all off balance. The compartment plunged into darkness, the lights flickering before dying completely. Panic erupted. Screams pierced the sudden silence as passengers struggled to regain their footing amid the falling debris. Ava felt a sharp pain in her leg, a searing agony that sent a jolt through her body.

Through the darkness, she heard Liam shout. "Ava! Get out! Now!"
He was pushing her towards a small emergency exit, a sliver of hope in the suffocating darkness. Ava struggled to her feet, her injured leg throbbing with pain. The compartment was filling with smoke; she could barely see a foot in front of her. Yet, Liam's urgency pushed her forward. He was distracting Seraphina's men.

She stumbled through the exit, crawling through the narrow corridor, the screams of the passengers fading behind her. As she reached the next car, the horrifying sight met her eyes. Liam, his body slumped against the wall, was surrounded by Seraphina's men. His eyes, wide and unseeing, stared up at the ceiling. He had bought her time. A sacrifice.

Ava was engulfed by a wave of grief, so intense it threatened to drown her. Liam, her unexpected ally, was dead. The weight of his sacrifice pressed down on her, a heavy burden she could barely bear. His death was not merely a loss, but a betrayal of the fragile hope she had clung to. The meticulously planned revenge had devolved into a brutal struggle for survival. And, in the ensuing chaos, she had been spared, while he had paid the ultimate price.

The guilt gnawed at her. She had been selfish, self-absorbed in her quest for vengeance. Liam had given his life to save her, a life she had thought she deserved. He had given his life for a woman she had come to respect and admire in the midst of chaos and violence.

She pressed on, driven now not just by revenge but by the heavy weight of Liam's sacrifice. His death fueled her determination, sharpening her focus, transforming her into a relentless force. She wasn't just fighting for herself anymore. She was fighting for Liam, for the life he had given.

Reaching the end of the car, she saw Elara, desperately trying to help the wounded. The young boy lay unconscious, his blood soaking through her jacket. She looked at Ava, her eyes filled with a mixture of relief and terror.

"We need to get out of here," Elara whispered, her voice strained. "The train is derailing."

The ground shook beneath them, the train swaying violently. Ava could hear the screech of metal against metal, a symphony of destruction. She knew they had only minutes. She had to find a way out, to save Elara and the young boy, and to ensure that Liam's sacrifice hadn't been in vain. The weight of responsibility fell upon her, a crushing weight of survival and the memory of Liam.

Their escape was a desperate dash through the wreckage of the train. Ava, fueled by adrenaline and a profound sense of loss, navigated the twisted metal and shattered glass, her injured leg forgotten. Elara, supporting the unconscious boy, followed close behind. They reached the front of the train, the air thick with smoke and the sound of tearing metal. They stumbled out onto the tracks, just as the train derailed, the world exploding around them.

They scrambled to safety, barely escaping the inferno. The aftermath was a scene of utter devastation, the screams of the survivors echoing against the night. The city, a distant hum until now, was a beacon of hope, its lights shimmering in the distance. They had survived. But the victory felt hollow, tainted by the bitter taste of loss. Liam's sacrifice had saved their lives, but it had left an unfillable void in their hearts. The relentless pursuit of justice, the meticulously planned revenge, had yielded a complicated truth: The cost of revenge, even when seemingly justified, is often measured in profound loss and irretrievable sacrifices.

The train lay broken, a twisted carcass of steel and shattered dreams. In the heart of Philadelphia, the city's lights cast a cold glow over the wreckage, a chilling reminder of the night's events and the heavy price they had paid. The journey to Philadelphia had ended, but the journey toward healing had just begun. A journey filled with guilt, grief, and the enduring legacy of a sacrifice that would forever change their lives. The moral ambiguity of their actions, the blur between victim and perpetrator, would remain with them, a constant companion in the long, hard road ahead. The echoes of the derailment, the screams of the injured, and the silent memory of Liam's sacrifice would continue to haunt their memories as the city lights faded into the rising dawn. Their victory, hard-earned and deeply tainted, was now theirs to carry.

The acrid smell of burning metal and smoke filled the air, a stark contrast to the crisp night air that had greeted them earlier. The mangled remains of the train lay scattered across the tracks like a discarded toy, a testament to the chaos that had unfolded. Sirens wailed in the distance, growing louder with each passing second, a harbinger of the impending scrutiny. Ava, Elara, and the unconscious boy were huddled together, the silence broken only by their ragged breaths and the distant screams of other survivors.

Elara's face, smudged with soot and streaked with tears, was etched with a mixture of relief and exhaustion. The boy, still unconscious, lay nestled in her lap, his breathing shallow but steady. Ava's injured leg throbbed with a dull, persistent pain, a minor inconvenience compared to the gaping hole Liam's death had left in her heart. The weight of his sacrifice pressed down on her, a crushing burden she was forced to carry amidst the pandemonium.

The first responders arrived, their faces grim as they surveyed the scene. The flashing lights of emergency vehicles cast a harsh, unforgiving glow on the devastation. Paramedics rushed to tend to the injured, their movements efficient and practiced, yet their faces betrayed the shock of the carnage. Police officers, their expressions stern and serious, began to cordon off the area, their voices sharp and authoritative as they questioned survivors.

Ava watched them, a detached observer in the midst of the unfolding chaos. The meticulously planned revenge, the carefully orchestrated scheme, had dissolved into a maelstrom of violence and unintended consequences. The clear lines she had drawn between victim and perpetrator, between right and wrong, were now hopelessly blurred. Liam's death, a sacrifice she could neither comprehend nor accept, had shattered her carefully constructed world, leaving her adrift in a sea of doubt and despair.

The initial interrogation was a blur of flashing lights, harsh questions, and the echoing sounds of sirens. They were taken to a nearby hospital, where the boy was treated for his injuries, while Ava and Elara were questioned separately. The police officers, while professional, were visibly shaken by the magnitude of the event. They were grappling with the sheer scale of the destruction and the complexity of the situation, a train hijacking that had quickly spiraled into a bloody free-for-all. The questions they asked were relentless, their intent to piece together the fragmented narrative of what had occurred on that ill-fated train to Philadelphia.

Ava recounted her story, carefully choosing her words, omitting certain details, embellishing others. She painted a picture of a young woman determined to exact justice, inadvertently caught in a crossfire, a victim of circumstance rather than the architect of the chaos. She spoke of Seraphina and her ruthlessness, but she carefully avoided mentioning her meticulously planned revenge scheme. It was a delicate balance, walking the tightrope between truth and self-preservation, between exposing her actions and shielding herself from the full weight of the law. The narrative she constructed was designed to evoke sympathy, to highlight her own victimhood while subtly obscuring the calculated nature of her actions.

Elara's testimony corroborated Ava's account, filling in the gaps, adding details that solidified Ava's narrative. She painted a picture of a chaotic struggle for survival, highlighting the bravery of certain individuals while minimizing the culpability of others. Together, their accounts presented a compelling narrative, a carefully constructed defense against the impending scrutiny.

The investigation dragged on for days, a slow and methodical process that unearthed the full horror of the event. The details of Seraphina's crimes were revealed, the extent of her ruthlessness exposed. But the investigation also unearthed other truths, truths that cast a darker shadow over the events on the train. The criminals involved were not merely corporate executives in disguise; they were part of a larger, more sinister organization, an intricate web of corruption that extended beyond the confines of the derailed train.

Ava, meanwhile, struggled with the emotional fallout. The guilt gnawed at her, a relentless and pervasive force that threatened to consume her. Liam's sacrifice cast a long shadow over her victory. The sense of justice she sought remained elusive, tainted by the brutal cost of its pursuit. The meticulously planned revenge had backfired spectacularly, leaving her with a profound sense of loss and the bitter realization that even the most carefully orchestrated plans could unravel in the face of unforeseen circumstances.

The media frenzy intensified. The story of the Philadelphia train derailment dominated headlines, captivating the public's attention with its gruesome details and dramatic twists. Ava, portrayed as both victim and perpetrator, found herself at the center of the media storm. She was hailed as a hero by some, condemned as a villain by others. The ambiguity of her actions, her own moral grayness, fueled endless speculation and debate.

As the investigation progressed, the authorities unearthed more intricate details about Seraphina's organization, a clandestine network extending its tentacles across multiple industries. The case became significantly larger than the initial train hijacking, evolving into a high-profile investigation involving multiple agencies and a vast network of accomplices.

The legal proceedings took months, dragging Ava further into the abyss of her grief and guilt. In the end, Seraphina and her associates were brought to justice, their crimes exposed to the world. However, the victory felt hollow, overshadowed by the heavy weight of loss. Liam's sacrifice served as a constant reminder of the price of revenge, the collateral damage inflicted in the relentless pursuit of justice.

Ava left Philadelphia, the city of broken dreams and shattered expectations, leaving behind the wreckage of the train and the ghosts of her past. She carried with her the heavy burden of Liam's sacrifice and the haunting knowledge of her own moral ambiguities. The journey toward healing was a long and arduous one, a path paved with grief, guilt, and the lingering question of whether the pursuit of justice was ever truly worth the price. The ambiguity remained, a constant companion in her silent reflection on the events, forever etched into her memory.

The courtroom was stifling, the air thick with the weight of unspoken accusations and simmering resentments. Ava sat rigidly in the spectator's gallery, her gaze fixed on Seraphina, who sat impeccably dressed, a picture of serene defiance. Seraphina, the mastermind behind the meticulously crafted web of deceit, the woman who had orchestrated the destruction of Ava's family, now faced the consequences of her actions. Yet, even in the face of impending incarceration, Seraphina exuded an aura of unsettling calm, a chilling indifference that sent shivers down Ava's spine.

The trial was a whirlwind of legal jargon, conflicting testimonies, and manipulative narratives. Ava had given her statement, carefully navigating the treacherous waters of truth and self-preservation. She had exposed Seraphina's crimes, detailing the elaborate scheme that had led to the train hijacking and the subsequent chaos. But she had also, subtly, defended herself, highlighting her own victimhood, the unintended consequences of her desperate attempt to avenge her family's destruction. The jury, a panel of impassive faces, seemed to hang on every word, their expressions inscrutable.

The prosecution presented a compelling case, meticulously piecing together the fragments of the events on the train. They showcased Seraphina's calculated ruthlessness, her intricate network of accomplices, and the devastating consequences of her actions. The defense, however, painted a different picture, casting doubt on the validity of certain testimonies, challenging the evidence, and portraying Seraphina as a victim of circumstance, a pawn in a larger game.

The verdict came as a relief, yet it felt hollow. Seraphina was found guilty on all counts, sentenced to a lengthy prison term. Justice, in a sense, had been served. But the victory tasted like ashes in Ava's mouth. The courtroom, now emptied of its tense energy, felt eerily silent. The weight of Liam's sacrifice pressed down on her, heavier than ever. His death, a senseless casualty in her pursuit of revenge, echoed in the quiet chambers, a constant reminder of the devastating cost of her actions.

The media circus that had surrounded the trial continued to swirl around Ava, casting a harsh spotlight on her life. She was depicted as both a hero and a villain, a tragic figure caught in a web of circumstance. Her actions were dissected, debated, and analyzed endlessly, fueling endless speculation and fueling moral ambiguities that lingered. The line between victim and perpetrator, once sharply defined in her mind, was now hopelessly blurred. The public devoured the stories, their thirst for sensational narratives insatiable.

The city of Philadelphia, once the stage for her carefully orchestrated revenge, had become a constant reminder of her loss. The city was a palimpsest of memories, every corner echoing with the ghosts of her past. She left, seeking solace in the anonymity of a new life, a new city far removed from the memories of the train derailment and the lingering weight of her actions. But the memories followed.

The years passed, slowly eroding the sharp edges of grief. The pain dulled, though it never truly disappeared, becoming a constant companion. She built a new life, but the echoes of the past remained. She found solace in helping others, using her experience to prevent similar tragedies. She became an advocate for victims of corporate greed and systemic injustices, channeling her pain into something positive, yet it was a subtle shift, a slow, deliberate process. The moral ambiguities remained, unresolved.

Then came the letter. An anonymous envelope, containing a single photograph. It showed a young girl, no older than ten, staring pensively at the ocean. The accompanying note was brief, cryptic: "Liam's daughter. He left her in my care." The unexpected revelation, a consequence of Ava's actions that she had never foreseen, struck her with the force of a physical blow. Liam's sacrifice had resulted not only in her own moral ambiguity, but in the unexpected legacy of a child he would never know. The weight of this newly discovered responsibility felt heavier than any burden she had carried before. The complexity of the consequences, now revealed, opened a new chapter of profound guilt and unexpected responsibility.

The ambiguous justice she had sought had been granted, yet the full weight of its cost continued to unfold, revealing unanticipated layers of pain and moral complexities. The end was not a definitive closure but a haunting realization: revenge, even when seemingly justified, comes with an inescapable price, a price that might extend beyond the immediate aftermath, reaching into unforeseen futures and unexpected lives. The pursuit of justice, she discovered, was a relentless journey, often leading to unexpected destinations, paved with unintended consequences, and forever imprinted with the lasting marks of moral ambiguities. The true nature of justice, she now understood, remained as elusive and complicated as the labyrinthine web of events that had led her to this point, leaving her to grapple with the endless complexities of morality, grief, and the enduring weight of her choices.

Chapter 5
Loose Ends

The screech of metal against metal, the lingering smell of smoke and fear – these were the immediate aftermath. The train, a mangled wreck, lay sprawled across the tracks just outside Philadelphia, a stark testament to the chaos that had unfolded within its confines. Emergency crews swarmed the scene, their red and blue lights flashing against the pre-dawn gloom, a cacophony of sirens cutting through the stunned silence. The air thrummed with a frenetic energy, a stark contrast to the claustrophobic terror that had held the passengers captive just hours before.

Inside the mangled carriages, the survivors huddled together, faces etched with shock and trauma. Whispers of near-misses and chilling encounters mingled with the groans of the injured. The metallic tang of blood mingled with the acrid scent of burnt plastic, creating a nauseating cocktail of horror and despair. Paramedics worked tirelessly, their skilled hands moving with practiced efficiency as they tended to the wounded, a grim ballet of life and death playing out amidst the wreckage.

The initial wave of panic gave way to a numb disbelief. The sheer scale of the disaster slowly sunk in, the full extent of the damage both physical and emotional, gradually revealed. The authorities, initially overwhelmed by the sheer volume of victims, moved into damage control. The investigation began immediately, a complex and painstaking process of gathering evidence, interviewing witnesses, and piecing together the shattered fragments of that nightmarish journey.

Meanwhile, the media descended upon the scene like vultures, their cameras flashing relentlessly, capturing every detail of the aftermath for eager consumption. The story of the hijacked train rapidly became national news, captivating audiences with its blend of suspense, intrigue, and tragedy. The airwaves buzzed with speculation, conjecture, and sensationalized accounts of the events, all vying for public attention. The city of Philadelphia, once a backdrop to Ava's meticulously planned revenge, found itself thrust into the unforgiving glare of the global spotlight.

The repercussions of the hijacking extended far beyond the immediate vicinity of the train wreck. The families of the victims, torn apart by grief and loss, struggled to cope with their devastating circumstances. The surviving passengers grappled with the psychological scars of the trauma, many suffering from nightmares, flashbacks, and crippling anxiety. Support groups and counseling services sprung into action, attempting to address the widespread mental health crisis that followed in the wake of the disaster.

Ava, having survived the ordeal and played a pivotal role in its resolution, found herself at the center of a media maelstrom. The newspapers splashed her image across their front pages, portraying her as both a hero and a villain. The public was divided. Some praised her for her bravery and resourcefulness, while others condemned her for instigating the events that had led to the train hijacking and the tragic loss of life. The moral ambiguities surrounding her actions fueled endless debate and speculation, turning her into a symbol of the complex issues surrounding justice, revenge, and the price of survival.

The city of Philadelphia itself seemed to bear the weight of the tragedy. The streets, usually bustling with life, seemed to echo with the ghost of the train's harrowing journey. The once-vibrant atmosphere felt heavy with a palpable sense of grief and uncertainty. The city was deeply affected, its rhythm disrupted by the ripple effects of the incident. The everyday life of its citizens was touched by the pervasive sense of unease, the memory of the chaos lingering in the collective consciousness. The usual celebratory buzz of the city, particularly noticeable around the train station, was dampened by a thick pall of somber reflection.

Ava found herself haunted by the echoes of the train's journey. Every whistle of a passing train, every glimpse of steel tracks, brought back the horrifying memories of that night. The city she once sought to conquer now served as a potent reminder of the devastating consequences of her actions. The places she had frequented – the restaurants, the coffee shops, even the park where she had planned her revenge – became imbued with a painful, indelible association to the catastrophe.

The investigation into the hijacking unearthed a vast network of corporate corruption and organized crime, revealing a layer of intrigue that extended far beyond Ava's initial plan. The intricate web of deceit and deception unraveled slowly, revealing the extent of Seraphina's power and reach. The authorities worked tirelessly to bring all those involved to justice, but the trail was winding, leading through dark corners of the city and into the shadowy world of international finance.

The aftermath also forced Ava to confront the ethical implications of her own actions. The line between victim and perpetrator, which she had once perceived as clear and distinct, was now blurred beyond recognition. Liam's sacrifice, a price paid for her quest for justice, cast a long shadow over her life, leaving an enduring sense of guilt and remorse. She realized the limitations of her simplistic pursuit of revenge, the unexpected and often tragic consequences that followed in its wake.

Despite the media's frenzy and the ongoing investigation, there were moments of quiet reflection. Ava found herself drawn to the quieter corners of the city, seeking solace in solitude. The Delaware River, flowing majestically past Philadelphia, provided a sense of calm amidst the chaos. She spent hours by the waterfront, watching the water ebb and flow, a silent witness to the city's grief and recovery.

She began to understand that true justice was not merely a matter of retribution, but of healing, reconciliation, and accountability. The journey towards that kind of justice was long and arduous, a process that would require confronting not just her enemies, but also the demons within herself. The aftermath was not a simple conclusion, but a new beginning, a challenging path that required confronting the weight of her actions and the complex morality at the heart of her story. The city of Philadelphia, once a stage for her vengeful scheme, now served as a reminder of the profound and enduring consequences of her choices. The lingering trauma, the media's insatiable hunger for details, and the unresolved moral ambiguities all created a dense, complex, and profoundly unsettling aftermath.

The investigation, far from being a swift resolution, became a labyrinthine journey into the city's underbelly. Detective Miller, a seasoned veteran with eyes that had seen too much, was leading the charge. He'd been haunted by the train wreck, not just by the sheer scale of the devastation, but by the unsettling ambiguity surrounding Ava's role. Was she a victim, a hero, or something far more complex? Miller wasn't sure, and that uncertainty fueled his relentless pursuit of the truth.

His investigation delved into the corporate world, a realm of polished veneers and hidden agendas. Seraphina Moreau, the elusive figure behind the criminal enterprise, remained a ghost, her influence felt but her presence unseen. Miller discovered a trail of meticulously crafted documents, offshore accounts, and coded messages, each piece leading him further down the rabbit hole. The intricate web of corruption extended far beyond the train hijacking, revealing a long-standing conspiracy reaching into the highest echelons of power.

Meanwhile, Ava, despite the media attention, retreated from the public eye. The accolades and condemnations meant little to her. The weight of Liam's sacrifice pressed heavily on her conscience. She found solace not in the city's glittering lights, but in the quiet solitude of her apartment, a stark contrast to the chaotic world she had inadvertently unleashed. She spent hours poring over Liam's journals, searching for clues, for answers, for some semblance of understanding. His words, filled with his dreams and anxieties, offered a poignant reminder of the life lost in the pursuit of justice.

Liam's journal entries revealed a deeper understanding of his motivations. He wasn't merely a pawn in Ava's revenge scheme; he was an active participant, driven by his own sense of justice, his own personal vendetta against Seraphina. His relationship with Ava, previously portrayed as a purely transactional partnership, unfolded as a complex tapestry of loyalty, affection, and shared trauma. His entries painted a picture of a man wrestling with his conscience, grappling with the moral implications of their plan, his doubts mirroring Ava's growing uncertainty.

The journal entries also revealed a previously unknown aspect of Seraphina's past, a connection to Ava's family that extended beyond the immediate events leading to their downfall. It was a revelation that turned the narrative on its head, adding layers of complexity to Ava's motivations and placing Seraphina's actions in a new and disturbing light. The seemingly clear-cut lines between victim and perpetrator dissolved into a gray landscape of shared pain and overlapping betrayals.

As Miller's investigation intensified, he unearthed a series of hidden transactions, linking Seraphina to a network of international arms dealers. The train hijacking, it turned out, was merely a small part of a much larger operation, a smokescreen for a far more sinister scheme. The evidence pointed to a conspiracy that threatened not just Philadelphia, but the stability of the nation as a whole.

Ava, having pieced together Liam's clues and the fragmented information from the police investigation, realized that Seraphina's reach was far greater than she had ever imagined. She also understood that simply bringing Seraphina down would not bring Liam back, nor would it truly bring justice to her family. She had to find a way to dismantle the entire network, to expose the intricate web of corruption that had allowed Seraphina to operate with such impunity.

This realization spurred Ava into action. She used her knowledge of Seraphina's operations, gleaned from Liam's journal and her own meticulous research, to create a new plan, a far more elaborate scheme than the one that had led to the train hijacking. This time, she wouldn't simply expose Seraphina; she would dismantle her empire, piece by piece, leaving no stone unturned.

Her strategy involved a carefully orchestrated series of leaks to the media, strategic alliances with unexpected allies, and a meticulous use of technology to expose Seraphina's network. She worked in the shadows, utilizing her skills as a hacker to expose incriminating evidence, while simultaneously staying one step ahead of the law. The lines between justice and lawlessness blurred even further as Ava's methods, though effective, were certainly unconventional.

The climax unfolded not in a dramatic courtroom showdown, but in a series of strategically timed revelations. News outlets exploded with reports of Seraphina's criminal activities, her empire crumbling under the weight of exposed evidence. The once-untouchable executive found herself facing a barrage of lawsuits, investigations, and international warrants. Her meticulously built facade shattered, revealing the ruthless pragmatism and cruel indifference at the heart of her empire.

The city of Philadelphia, initially shocked by the aftermath of the train hijacking, found itself celebrating a different kind of victory. Seraphina's downfall was not only a symbol of justice served, but also a testament to the resilience of a community shaken but not broken. The weight of the tragedy still lingered, but the sense of collective trauma was tempered by the triumph of unveiling a deep-seated web of corruption.

Ava, having achieved her goal, faced a different kind of reckoning. The media painted her as a hero, but the public's perception remained divided. Some celebrated her audacity and effectiveness; others condemned her morally ambiguous methods. Ava, however, found a measure of peace in the knowledge that she had brought down a powerful criminal and dismantled a vast network of corruption. She understood that true justice was a complex endeavor, a long and winding road that demanded a level of moral ambiguity she was forced to navigate.

The epilogue found Ava far from the spotlight, starting a new life in a quiet, undisclosed location. The trauma lingered, the memories of the train hijacking and Liam's death forever etched in her soul. But the city of Philadelphia, the stage for her grand scheme and the symbol of her loss, was no longer the source of her pain. It was instead a testament to her resilience, a reminder of the journey she undertook and the sacrifices made along the way. Her tale remained a complex, morally ambiguous narrative, leaving the reader pondering the fine line between justice and revenge, and the enduring price of both. The city, once haunted by the echoes of a mangled train, gradually began to heal, its rhythm restored, the memory of the ordeal slowly fading into the collective consciousness. The tale of the hijacked train, a story of revenge, survival, and redemption, became a dark parable whispered amongst its citizens, a cautionary tale of the high cost of justice and the elusive nature of true reconciliation.

The silence in her apartment was a stark contrast to the cacophony of the media frenzy that had followed the unraveling of Seraphina Moreau's empire. Ava sat bathed in the pale glow of her laptop screen, the city lights a blurry reflection in the glass. The victory felt hollow, a bitter taste lingering on her tongue. She had achieved what she set out to do, dismantling a vast criminal network and bringing down a woman who had destroyed her family, but the price had been far steeper than she anticipated. Liam's absence was a gaping wound, a constant ache in her chest. His face, etched in her memory, haunted her waking hours and invaded her dreams.

The media hailed her as a hero, a modern-day vigilante who brought down a corrupt empire. Articles painted her as a brilliant strategist, a technological prodigy, a woman who had single-handedly exposed a vast conspiracy. But the accolades felt like epitaphs, hollow pronouncements over a life irrevocably changed. The celebration was for the city, for the justice served, but Ava felt nothing but a profound emptiness. The cheers were distant echoes in a world that had grown silent around her.

She reread Liam's journal, the words blurring through her tears. His entries weren't just accounts of their meticulously planned operation; they were intimate glimpses into his soul, his fears, his doubts. She saw the man she loved, not as a tool in her revenge, but as a partner, a confidant, a soul bound to hers by shared trauma and a desperate yearning for justice. His last entry, a testament to his unwavering love and his growing apprehension, felt like a final goodbye. The words were a poignant reminder of the human cost of their actions, the irreparable damage inflicted in the name of retribution.

The weight of Liam's sacrifice pressed heavily on her conscience. She had lost him, not in a dramatic confrontation with Seraphina, but in the intricate dance of deception and danger that they had orchestrated. It wasn't a clean kill; it was a messy, agonizing death, a sacrifice made for a cause that had grown increasingly ambiguous. The thrill of victory had evaporated, leaving behind a chilling realization: she had traded one kind of pain for another, a profound and enduring loss that no amount of media praise could ever alleviate.

Sleep offered no escape. Nightmares plagued her, vivid replays of the train hijacking, the chaos, the screams, the terrifying realization of their near-miss. She would wake up in a cold sweat, her heart pounding in her chest, the memory of Liam's lifeless body etched into her mind. Therapy offered little solace. The therapists, trained professionals accustomed to dealing with trauma, were ill-equipped to handle the specific horror of her experience, the moral ambiguity of her actions, the overwhelming grief of her loss.

The lines between justice and revenge had blurred beyond recognition. She had sought justice for her family, but in the pursuit, she had crossed ethical boundaries, compromised her values, and ultimately, paid the ultimate price. Her quest for revenge had been meticulously planned, surgically executed, but the emotional fallout was a devastating aftermath. The psychological toll was far-reaching, a deep-seated wound that cut through her soul.

The solitude, initially a refuge, became a prison. The apartment, once a sanctuary, now felt like a mausoleum, filled with the ghost of Liam's presence. She found herself avoiding places that held memories, avoiding conversations that might trigger painful reminiscences. The city, once a backdrop to her meticulously planned revenge, had become a constant reminder of her loss. The streets, the buildings, the faces of strangers - all seemed to echo with the absence of Liam.

She tried to find solace in her work, delving into complex coding projects, hoping to lose herself in the intricate logic of algorithms. But the code, once a source of comfort and intellectual stimulation, now felt sterile, emotionless, a stark contrast to the messy reality of her life. The digital world, once her sanctuary, offered no escape from the crushing weight of her grief and guilt.

The investigation into Seraphina's network continued, its tentacles reaching into the highest echelons of power. The revelations were staggering, exposing a web of corruption that extended beyond the city, the nation, even reaching into international spheres of influence. The fall of Seraphina was only the beginning, the tip of an iceberg of deceit and depravity. The city, initially stunned by the revelation, had gradually begun to heal, but the ripples of the scandal would continue to reverberate for years to come.

Ava, despite the media's portrayal, remained a recluse. She understood the value of her anonymity, the necessity of staying out of the limelight. The public's perception of her was as conflicted as her own self-assessment. She was a hero to some, a ruthless vigilante to others. The truth, as always, lay somewhere in between. She had brought down a vast criminal network, but at a devastating personal cost.

She sought not redemption, but reconciliation, a way to make peace with her loss and the morally ambiguous choices she had made. The journey was long, arduous, filled with moments of despair and fleeting glimmers of hope. The path to healing was not linear, but a winding road, fraught with emotional pitfalls and unexpected detours. The price of revenge, she realized, was not just the loss of a loved one, but the enduring psychological toll, the permanent scar etched onto the soul. The memory of Liam, the pain of his loss, would forever be a part of her story, a constant reminder of the steep cost of seeking justice. The city might heal, but her wounds would remain, a constant, painful reminder of the dark path she had traveled. The quest for revenge had ended, but the journey of self-forgiveness had only just begun.

The city hummed with a false sense of peace. The arrest of Seraphina Moreau, the dismantling of her empire, had been splashed across every news outlet, celebrated as a triumph of justice. But Ava knew the truth was far more nuanced, far more brutal. The headlines lauded her as a hero, a modern-day Joan of Arc, but the accolades felt like salt rubbed into a festering wound. The victory was hollow, the taste of it ash in her mouth. She had destroyed Seraphina's empire, yes, but at what cost?

Liam's absence was a gaping hole in her life, a constant reminder of the price she had paid. His death wasn't a glorious battle; it was a cold, calculated consequence of their meticulously planned operation. The train heist, initially a brilliant maneuver, had spiraled into a chaotic free-for-all. The hijacking by a separate criminal syndicate—a twist Ava hadn't foreseen—turned the planned takedown into a desperate fight for survival. The lines between victim and perpetrator blurred, dissolving into a maelstrom of violence and betrayal.

She replayed the events in her mind, a relentless loop of horrifying images: the screams, the gunfire, the desperate scramble for safety amid the chaos. Liam, shielding her from a hail of bullets, his lifeblood staining the grimy train floor. She had witnessed his death, a slow, agonizing fade as the adrenaline wore off and the reality of the situation slammed into her. His final words, muffled by the din of the hijacking, still echoed in her ears—a whispered promise of love, a silent goodbye.

The investigation's aftermath offered little solace. While Seraphina's network had been exposed, revealing a vast conspiracy that reached the highest echelons of power, the justice served felt incomplete. The arrests, the convictions, felt almost trivial compared to the immeasurable loss she had suffered. It wasn't just Liam's life; it was the loss of their shared future, the stolen dreams, the unspoken promises. The future they had envisioned, a future where they could rebuild their lives, free from the shadow of Seraphina, had been cruelly snatched away.

The media painted her as a brilliant strategist, a technological marvel, a lone wolf fighting against impossible odds. They celebrated her courage, her intelligence, her unwavering dedication to justice. But Ava saw only the broken pieces of herself, the shattered fragments of her life, mirroring the devastation she had unleashed. The victory was overshadowed by the profound grief that consumed her, a grief that no amount of praise could alleviate.

Sleep offered no escape. Nightmares relentlessly pursued her, vivid re-enactments of the train hijacking, the blood, the chaos, the terror of Liam's dying breath. She woke up drenched in sweat, her heart hammering against her ribs, her mind replaying every agonizing detail. Therapy sessions became a blur of fragmented memories and choked sobs, leaving her feeling more lost and isolated than ever. The therapists, while skilled in their profession, seemed unable to grasp the specific nature of her trauma—the moral ambiguity of her actions, the agonizing weight of her grief.

The question of justice echoed in her mind, a relentless tormentor. Had she truly achieved justice for her family? Or had her pursuit of revenge merely replaced one kind of pain with another? She had brought down a criminal empire, but at the cost of her own happiness, her own sanity. The line between justice and revenge had blurred, dissolving into a murky wasteland of guilt and self-recrimination.

The initial sense of accomplishment had quickly morphed into a profound sense of emptiness. The city celebrated its newfound freedom from Seraphina's reign of terror, but Ava felt nothing but a profound, gnawing loss. The victory was tainted, poisoned by the irreversible consequences of her actions. She had sought justice, but in the process, she had destroyed herself.

The investigation continued, exposing the rot that festered beneath the surface of the city's veneer of respectability. But Ava remained detached, a silent observer of the unfolding events. She had retreated into herself, burying herself in her work, finding solace in the cold logic of algorithms, in the precision of code. But even the digital world, once her refuge, offered no escape from the emotional turmoil that consumed her.

The city healed, but Ava's wounds remained open, raw and bleeding. She had inflicted a devastating blow on Seraphina Moreau, a blow that resonated through the city's elite and beyond. Yet, the cost had been immeasurable. She had achieved justice, perhaps, but at the expense of everything that mattered. The city's applause faded into the background noise of her own suffering; the echoes of the train's whistle, a constant reminder of the price of revenge. The question of justice was no longer a simple equation; it was a complex, agonizing riddle with no clear solution, a testament to the brutal reality that sometimes, even victory can feel like defeat. And in the silent chambers of her heart, Ava knew the true price of justice had been far too high.

The rain lashed against the windows of her apartment, mirroring the storm raging within her. The city lights blurred into indistinct streaks, mirroring the confusion in her mind. Weeks bled into months, the rhythm of her life a monotonous cycle of work, therapy, and the gnawing emptiness that had become her constant companion. The accolades, the praise, the fleeting moments of public recognition—they were all meaningless now, hollow echoes in the vast cavern of her grief.

She had sought justice, and she had found it, in a way. Seraphina Moreau was behind bars, her empire in ruins, her reign of terror finally over. But the victory felt like a pyrrhic one, a hollow triumph achieved at an exorbitant cost. Liam was gone, his absence a gaping wound that refused to heal, a constant ache in her chest that no amount of medication or therapy could soothe.

She found herself drawn to the waterfront, the relentless rhythm of the waves a stark contrast to the stillness of her apartment. The salty air stung her eyes, but it was a welcome sensation, a physical reminder that she was still alive, still breathing, still capable of feeling, even if the feelings were mostly pain. The vast expanse of the ocean mirrored the immensity of her loss, a reminder of the boundless nature of grief.

She thought about the future, a concept that once held so much promise, now fraught with uncertainty. Before, the future had been a clear path, a linear progression towards a shared life with Liam, a life free from the shadow of Seraphina Moreau. Now, the future stretched before her, a vast and unknown territory, treacherous and uncharted. The path ahead was unclear, shrouded in mist, with no guarantee of safe passage.

The therapist had suggested focusing on self-care, on rebuilding her life, on finding a new purpose. But the words felt hollow, a prescribed remedy for a malady far too complex, far too deeply rooted in her soul. The suggestion seemed trivial, a simplistic solution to a problem of immense complexity. The pain ran too deep, the wounds too profound.

She started small. She began to cook again, finding a strange solace in the precise measurements, the methodical process, the transformation of raw ingredients into something nourishing and comforting. She rediscovered her love for music, finding solace in the melodic strains of Chopin and the soaring vocals of Ella Fitzgerald. She slowly re-engaged with her friends, hesitantly at first, then with increasing openness, finding comfort in their shared silence and unspoken understanding.

Her work, once a refuge, had become a source of both solace and torment. The intricate algorithms, the precise code, offered a temporary escape from the overwhelming weight of her emotions, but also served as a constant reminder of the task that had consumed her, a reminder of the price she had paid.

One evening, she stumbled upon an old photograph of her and Liam, taken on a trip to the coast. The picture was filled with light, laughter, and unbridled joy. A wave of bittersweet memories washed over her, a poignant reminder of the happiness they had shared, of the future they had envisioned. The memories were both a source of pain and a source of strength. The pain was sharp, raw, and visceral; but the strength it ignited felt profound, an untamed force buried deep within her soul.

The tears flowed freely this time, not as a sign of defeat, but as a release, a cathartic cleansing. The dam had broken, and the floodgates opened, washing away years of suppressed grief, leaving behind a space for healing, a space for growth, a space for a new beginning.

She started to explore new interests, to challenge herself, to step outside of her comfort zone. She took a pottery class, finding a unexpected serenity in the tactile process of shaping clay. She volunteered at a local animal shelter, finding comfort in the unconditional love of the abandoned creatures. She slowly began to re-engage with the world, but on her own terms, at her own pace.

The process was slow, painstaking, and at times agonizing. The path to healing was not linear, not predictable, not without setbacks. There were days when the grief threatened to overwhelm her again, days when the memories of Liam's death felt unbearably sharp. But she learned to navigate these moments, to find strength in her vulnerability, to embrace the messy, imperfect process of healing.

The city continued to buzz with life, oblivious to her private struggle. But Ava's world had shifted, had transformed. The raw edges of her pain had begun to soften, the sharp corners of her grief had begun to smooth. She was still scarred, still bearing the weight of her past, but she was no longer defined by it. She had faced the darkness, and she had emerged, battered but not broken.

The question of justice, once a burning question, had faded into the background, replaced by a new question: what now? What kind of future did she want to build? What kind of life did she want to live? The answers were not clear, but the very act of asking the questions felt like a step forward, a sign of her growing resilience.

She started to see possibilities, glimpses of a future that wasn't defined by loss, but by hope, by resilience, by the quiet strength that she had discovered within herself. She was no longer the young woman consumed by revenge; she was a survivor, a woman who had faced unimaginable hardship and emerged stronger, more compassionate, and more determined to find her own path, her own purpose, her own happiness. The new chapter was not written yet, but the blank page held the promise of a future filled with possibilities, a future that was entirely her own. The train had left the station, carrying its cargo of memories and regrets, but Ava was stepping onto a new platform, ready to board a new train, heading towards an uncertain but hopeful destination. The future remained unwritten, a blank page awaiting the strokes of her pen, but this time, the story would be her own.

Chapter 6
Epilogue

The rhythmic click of the train wheels on the tracks had become a lullaby, a monotonous drone that lulled her into a state of uneasy calm. The aftermath of the train hijacking had been a blur of media attention, interrogations, and hushed whispers. She had given her statement to the authorities, recounted the harrowing events of that night, the chaos, the fear, the desperate fight for survival. But even as she spoke, a nagging unease gnawed at her. Something didn't quite fit.

She'd seen the faces of the hijackers, their cold, calculating eyes, their ruthless efficiency. They were professionals, highly trained and expertly organized. The precision of their movements, the flawless execution of their plan, left no room for doubt. They were not mere criminals; they were something... more.

It was in the days following the incident, sifting through the fragmented memories, the blurry images, the echoes of shouted orders and panicked screams, that a detail surfaced, a detail that had been buried under the weight of trauma and adrenaline. A fleeting glimpse, a snatched image, a single word spoken in a hushed voice in the tense darkness of the hijacked car. It was a name: "Project Nightingale."

The phrase echoed in her mind, a discordant note in the

symphony of chaos. Project Nightingale. The name held a chilling resonance, a whisper of something clandestine, something deeply unsettling. It sparked a memory, a faint echo from her research into Seraphina Moreau, a name she'd almost forgotten, buried beneath the avalanche of events that had followed. There had been whispers, rumors, hints of a shadowy organization, a clandestine project shrouded in secrecy. Project Nightingale. Could it be?

Driven by a desperate need for answers, Ava plunged back into her research, poring over old files, rereading forgotten reports, following every tenuous thread of information. She unearthed encrypted messages, coded communications, cryptic references hidden within seemingly innocuous documents. Slowly, painstakingly, a picture began to emerge, a chilling mosaic of interconnected events, hidden agendas, and long-forgotten conspiracies.

Project Nightingale, she discovered, was not just a name; it was a vast, intricate network of power, a clandestine operation involving influential figures across various sectors: politics, finance, even the military. Seraphina Moreau had been just one piece of this intricate puzzle, a pawn in a far larger game. The train hijacking, Ava realized with dawning horror, hadn't been a random act of violence; it had been a carefully orchestrated event, a strategic maneuver in a much larger conflict.

The hijackers, the ruthless professionals who had held her captive, were not mere criminals. They were agents, operatives, highly trained individuals acting on orders from a shadowy organization. And the supposed corporate executives they impersonated were far from ordinary businesspeople. They were high-ranking members of Project Nightingale itself, people who held immense power, influence, and a deadly secret.

The revelation hit her like a physical blow. The justice she had sought, the revenge she had believed she had achieved, was nothing but a distraction, a carefully constructed illusion meant to conceal a far greater truth. Seraphina Moreau had been a scapegoat, a sacrificial lamb offered up to protect the true architects of the vast conspiracy.

The pieces began to fall into place, connecting seemingly unrelated incidents, explaining coincidences she had dismissed as mere chance. She saw connections now between the financial scandals, the political cover-ups, the inexplicable disappearances she'd stumbled upon during her investigation. They were all pieces of a larger, far more sinister puzzle, all interconnected facets of Project Nightingale's intricate network.

The revelation was not only disturbing but terrifying. It exposed a level of corruption, a depth of depravity that stretched far beyond her initial understanding. The individuals involved were not just criminals; they were powerful, influential figures, people who wielded tremendous power and who would stop at nothing to protect their secrets. She had become entangled in something far beyond her comprehension, a conspiracy so vast and intricate that it could topple governments and rewrite history.

The weight of this newfound knowledge bore down on her, crushing her with its sheer magnitude. The victory she had celebrated was now tainted, hollow, a fleeting moment of relief in the face of an overwhelming reality. Her sense of justice, once a guiding principle, was now fractured, shattered into a thousand pieces. The lines between right and wrong had blurred, obscured by the intricate web of deception and betrayal.

Sleep became an elusive luxury, replaced by a relentless cycle of research, analysis, and sleepless nights spent piecing together the fragmented puzzle. She revisited her memories of the night on the train, searching for new clues, interpreting events through the lens of her new understanding. The faces of the hijackers, the subtle cues, the whispered conversations, all took on a new significance.

She realized the carefully planned diversions, the misleading clues laid by the hijackers, and the carefully constructed narratives spun by Seraphina Moreau had been designed to conceal the true nature of the operation. The chaos on the train had been a carefully orchestrated distraction, a smokescreen designed to draw attention away from the true goal of Project Nightingale.

The more she discovered, the more she realized the true extent of the danger she was in. She was no longer just a witness; she had become a target. Project Nightingale would stop at nothing to silence her, to protect its secrets. Her life was in immediate danger, a fact that hit her with the force of a physical blow.

The question now was not just about seeking justice, but about survival. The line between victim and perpetrator had blurred, but one thing remained clear: she had to expose the truth, no matter the cost. The weight of responsibility rested heavily on her shoulders, a crushing burden. But she would not yield. She would not be silenced.

The final piece of the puzzle came from an unexpected source: an anonymous package arrived at her doorstep, containing a single flash drive. Inside, she found a video recording, a confession from one of the high-ranking members of Project Nightingale, a man who had grown weary of the organization's dark deeds and decided to confess before it was too late. The video detailed the organization's history, its goals, its members, and its long-term plans, painting a chilling picture of global manipulation and control. It was the final, irrefutable proof of everything she had suspected.

With this evidence, she knew what she had to do. The game was far from over. This was not simply revenge; it was a fight for the very fabric of truth and justice, a struggle against the dark forces that had for too long held the reins of power. The fight was far from over; in fact, it had only just begun. She had played her hand, a winning hand. Now she only had to play it right. The train had reached its destination, but her journey had only just begun. The epilogue was yet to be written.

The anonymous confession, while providing irrefutable evidence of Project Nightingale's existence and its insidious reach, also raised more questions than it answered. The video, grainy and poorly lit, showed a haggard man, his face etched with regret and fear, confessing his involvement in a conspiracy so vast it was almost incomprehensible. He named names, revealed locations, detailed operations, yet the full picture remained elusive, shrouded in a fog of half-truths and deliberate omissions. His confession felt incomplete, as if a crucial piece of the puzzle was still missing, a vital link yet to be discovered.

Ava found herself haunted by the man's final words, a whispered plea for forgiveness that echoed in the silence of her apartment. His repentance felt hollow, almost performative, a desperate attempt to absolve himself of his guilt without truly revealing the extent of his culpability. He'd implicated others, certainly, but he'd shielded himself, carefully navigating the treacherous waters of confession, revealing just enough to implicate others, yet saving his own skin. Was his confession genuine, or was it a calculated move, a carefully crafted deception designed to protect himself while sacrificing others? The question gnawed at her, fueling her already burning desire for answers.
The media frenzy that followed the release of the video was predictable, yet the ensuing fallout was far from straightforward. While Project Nightingale's existence was undeniable, the intricate web of its operations remained largely obscured. Investigations were

launched, arrests were made, but the real power brokers remained elusive, their identities hidden behind a wall of legal maneuvering and carefully cultivated public image. The public, captivated by the sensational details of the confession, seemed more interested in the drama than the underlying truth. Ava watched it all unfold with a mixture of frustration and growing unease. The victory felt pyrrhic.

She replayed the video countless times, analyzing every frame, every nuance of the confessor's expression, searching for hidden meanings, for clues the authorities had missed. She focused on the subtle body language, the barely perceptible hesitations in his speech, the fleeting glances toward unseen corners of the room. She suspected the presence of hidden cameras, unseen observers, a carefully staged confession designed to mislead. The man's confession felt less like a genuine act of remorse and more like a carefully orchestrated act of self-preservation. The question of his true motives lingered, a persistent shadow in the aftermath of his revelation.

The authorities, hampered by bureaucratic red tape and political interference, were moving slowly, their investigation painstaking and frustratingly slow. Ava, however, felt the urgency of time. Project Nightingale was not dormant; it was adapting, reorganizing, waiting for the storm to pass before striking again. She knew she couldn't rely on official channels; she had to act independently, to uncover the remaining pieces of the puzzle, to expose the true architects of this vast conspiracy.

Her own past caught up with her. The shadow of her family's destruction, the burning desire for revenge that had initially driven her, resurfaced, amplified by this newly discovered level of corruption. It was no longer about personal vengeance; it was about preventing future catastrophes, about preventing Project Nightingale from ever again unleashing its deadly agenda upon the world. But the line between personal justice and wider societal implications blurred, leaving her questioning her own motives, and wondering if she was even capable of objectively investigating this network that reached the very top of the societal ladder.

The deeper she delved into the conspiracy, the more she realized the impossibility of her task. The individuals involved were not merely criminals; they were the architects of global power structures, their influence spreading through every level of society, their tentacles reaching into every corner of the world. Exposing them would not be a simple matter of revealing a few names and locations; it would require unraveling a tangled web of financial transactions, political alliances, and covert operations that spanned decades.

The anonymity of the confession also troubled her. Who was the source? Was it an inside man, a whistleblower acting out of conscience, or a double agent attempting to redirect attention away from the true perpetrators? The very act of sending the flash drive posed its own set of questions. How had the sender managed to bypass the security surrounding the organization? And how could they guarantee their own safety, after such a brazen act of defiance? The anonymity, while offering protection, also created an impenetrable wall of secrecy, which ultimately hindered her investigations.

Sleep offered little respite. Nights were filled with the rhythmic clicking of her laptop keyboard, the flickering glow of the computer screen illuminating her face as she sifted through mountains of data, deciphering coded messages, tracking financial transactions, and piecing together fragments of information gathered from various sources. Days were spent navigating the treacherous waters of the political landscape, cautiously approaching potential allies, and carefully managing the risks. The constant threat of exposure hung over her, a persistent shadow that followed her every step.

The emotional toll was immense. The weight of the responsibility she carried, the sheer scale of the conspiracy she was fighting, the constant threat to her own safety—it all combined to create an overwhelming pressure. Yet, despite the exhaustion, the fear, and the uncertainty, she continued, driven by a relentless determination to expose the truth, no matter the personal cost. The epilogue left a bitter taste in her mouth, a sense of victory tarnished by the overwhelming size and complexity of what she had uncovered. She had won a battle, but the war, she knew, was far from over. The lingering questions, unanswered and unsettling, served as a grim reminder of the immense power and reach of Project Nightingale, a reminder that justice, even in the face of overwhelming evidence, might remain elusive. The train had reached its destination, but the journey—her journey—had only just begun. The final chapter, the ultimate resolution, remained unwritten, a chilling testament to the enduring power of secrecy and the enduring fight for truth.

The train's arrival in Philadelphia felt anticlimactic, a stark contrast to the frantic energy that had consumed the journey. The city's lights, usually a vibrant spectacle, seemed muted, their brilliance dulled by the lingering tension that clung to Ava like a second skin. The authorities swarmed the train, their efficiency a stark contrast to the sluggishness of their earlier investigation.

The passengers, a mixture of shaken survivors and relieved witnesses, were shepherded away, their faces a canvas of shock and disbelief. Ava, however, remained, her gaze fixed on the empty seats, each one a silent testament to the chaos that had unfolded.

The immediate aftermath was a blur of interrogations, statements, and medical examinations. The media frenzy intensified, transforming the train into a symbol of both terror and resilience. Ava found herself thrust into the spotlight, her image plastered across newspapers and television screens. She was hailed as a hero, a courageous woman who had single-handedly exposed a vast criminal conspiracy. But the accolades felt hollow, a superficial recognition that failed to address the deeper complexities of her actions.

The justice she had sought, the revenge she had craved, seemed to have dissolved into a murky ambiguity. The criminals were apprehended, their involvement in Project Nightingale irrefutable. Yet, the victory felt incomplete, tainted by the knowledge that the true architects of the conspiracy remained at large. Their influence, she realized, extended far beyond the reach of the law. The network was vast, its tendrils reaching into the highest echelons of power. Exposing them would require more than a single act of defiance; it would require a sustained campaign, a relentless pursuit of truth that challenged the very foundations of the established order.

Her own morality was thrown into sharp relief. The line between victim and perpetrator had blurred beyond recognition during the train hijacking. She had manipulated events, using deception and coercion to achieve her goals. Had she become what she sought to destroy? The question haunted her, forcing her to confront the ethical implications of her actions. Was her pursuit of justice justified, even if it involved compromising her own integrity?

The anonymous confession, while pivotal in exposing Project Nightingale, raised further questions about the nature of truth and the reliability of information. The man's remorse, or lack thereof, left Ava with a sense of unease. Had he truly repented, or had he simply sought to protect himself by sacrificing others? The act of confession itself was a carefully orchestrated performance, a calculated move designed to manipulate the narrative and shift the focus away from the real perpetrators.

The media, focused on the sensational aspects of the story, failed to delve into the deeper complexities of the conspiracy. The public, captivated by the drama, seemed indifferent to the lingering questions of accountability and systemic corruption. Ava found herself increasingly isolated, her concerns dismissed as the ramblings of a traumatized witness. She was left to grapple with the implications of her actions, her pursuit of justice turning into a lonely odyssey.

The epilogue wasn't a triumphant conclusion, but rather a contemplation on the enduring nature of power and the fragility of justice. The train journey had been a microcosm of the larger societal struggles, a claustrophobic setting where the boundaries between good and evil, victim and perpetrator, were constantly shifting. Ava's fight for justice had been a testament to human resilience, a fierce struggle against overwhelming odds. Yet, it also revealed the limitations of individual action in the face of systemic corruption and pervasive influence.

The feeling of closure was elusive. The sense of accomplishment was overshadowed by the sheer scale of the corruption she had uncovered. The individuals she had brought to justice were merely pawns in a far larger game, and their capture did little to dismantle the network. Their removal, in fact, could even cause a realignment of power, leading to an even more dangerous outcome.

Sleep was a distant memory, replaced by a restless energy that propelled her forward. She knew that the fight was far from over. Project Nightingale, resilient and adaptive, would regroup, reform, and emerge again in a new form, its network reorganized and its operations more subtle. She had won a battle, a significant one, but the war continued, a relentless struggle against a foe that operated in the shadows.

The burden of knowledge weighed heavily on her. She was no longer just a victim seeking revenge; she was a guardian against a formidable threat. The lines between her personal quest for justice and her responsibility to the world blurred, culminating in a profound sense of loneliness. She had allies, certainly, but the trust had to be earned, not given, and the lines of loyalty could shift as quickly as the tides. The depth of the conspiracy stretched further than she had initially anticipated, implicating individuals in positions of power who seemed untouchable.

The anonymity of the confessor continued to haunt her. Was he a true whistleblower, or a double agent playing a long game? The question had become inextricably linked with her own journey. The more she delved into the matter, the more she realized that the answer held clues to the organization's inner workings and future operations. Understanding the motivation behind the anonymous confession was critical to preventing future incidents and dismantling the network completely.

The unanswered questions echoed in the silence of her apartment, the rhythmic tapping of her keyboard a constant reminder of the work that lay ahead. Each clue, each piece of information, was another step closer to unraveling the truth, but the path remained fraught with danger and uncertainty. The fight for justice was a relentless pursuit, demanding unwavering commitment, even in the face of overwhelming adversity. The train ride had reached its conclusion, but her journey, a complex and challenging odyssey, was only just beginning. The ending was not a triumphant celebration, but a stark reminder of the ongoing fight against injustice, a fight in which even victory felt bittersweet. The ultimate question remained: how could she, a single individual, confront a system so vast, so deeply entrenched, so utterly corrupt? The answer, like the path ahead, remained shrouded in uncertainty.

The weight of her choices pressed down on Ava like the crushing weight of the city itself, a tangible force that seeped into her bones and chilled her to the core. Philadelphia, once a symbol of her hoped-for triumph, now felt like a cage, its imposing skyline a constant reminder of the unfinished business that gnawed at her conscience. The media frenzy, initially a source of validation, had quickly morphed into a suffocating blanket of expectations, demands for closure, and an insatiable hunger for a neatly packaged narrative that simply didn't exist. The truth, she realized, was messy, fragmented, and far more terrifying than any simplistic account could convey.

The arrests, the public pronouncements, the seemingly swift resolution – it was all a carefully constructed façade. Beneath the surface, the tendrils of Project Nightingale continued to spread, their reach extending far beyond the grasp of the law. The individuals she had exposed were merely expendable pieces, readily sacrificed to protect the true architects of the conspiracy. Their removal had created a vacuum, a power void that would inevitably be filled, likely by individuals even more ruthless and cunning. The system, she understood with chilling clarity, was self-healing, its inherent corruption too deeply entrenched to be eradicated by a single, dramatic act of defiance.

Sleep offered no respite. Even in her dreams, the speeding train lurched and swayed, the cries of the hostages echoing in the darkness. The faces of those she had unwittingly involved, the men and women caught in the crossfire of her desperate plan, haunted her waking hours. She saw their fear, their vulnerability, reflected in the flickering city lights outside her window. The guilt was a constant companion, a relentless shadow that clung to her every move. Had she really achieved justice, or had she simply traded one form of suffering for another?

The anonymous confession, the key that had unlocked the door to Project Nightingale, remained a source of profound unease. The confessor's motivations remained a mystery, a riddle wrapped in an enigma. Was he a repentant sinner seeking redemption, a double agent playing a dangerous game, or a pawn in a far larger, more intricate scheme? The ambiguity gnawed at her, fueling a relentless need to uncover the truth behind his actions. The more she investigated, the more she realized the confession was not a simple act of contrition, but a carefully calibrated move designed to shift the focus, to redirect blame, and to protect those truly responsible.

Her investigation led her down a rabbit hole of cryptic messages, coded communications, and shadowed figures operating just beyond the reach of the law. She uncovered hidden accounts, offshore corporations, and shell companies, all part of a vast network designed to launder money and obscure the true source of the organization's funding. The scale of the operation was breathtaking, the web of deceit so complex it threatened to overwhelm her.

She found herself relying on unexpected allies – disillusioned government officials, disgruntled former employees, and even a former rival, a woman whose life had been irrevocably damaged by Project Nightingale. These unlikely alliances were forged in shared trauma and a mutual desire for accountability. But the trust was fragile, constantly tested by the betrayals and manipulations that had become the norm. The lines of loyalty shifted as readily as the wind, making every interaction a calculated risk.

The city itself seemed to conspire against her, its labyrinthine streets and shadows mirroring the complexity of the conspiracy. She felt watched, pursued, her every move monitored. Paranoia, a constant companion, became her most reliable ally, sharpening her instincts and heightening her awareness of potential threats. She learned to trust her intuition, a sixth sense honed by years of navigating danger.

Her quest for justice had morphed into something far more profound – a crusade against an enemy that seemed invincible. She was no longer simply seeking revenge for her family; she was fighting for the future, for a world free from the insidious influence of corrupt power. The personal stakes had been irrevocably intertwined with a larger fight for truth and accountability.

The weight of her knowledge was immense, a burden she carried with a fierce determination. Each piece of information she uncovered, each clue she followed, brought her closer to the truth, but it also amplified the risks. The closer she got, the more dangerous the game became. The individuals at the top of Project Nightingale were not merely criminals; they were architects of a system that permeated every level of society. They wielded influence and power that seemed untouchable.

She spent countless nights poring over documents, sifting through encrypted data, piecing together fragmented clues. The sheer volume of information was overwhelming, but she pressed on, driven by an unwavering determination to expose the truth. The city became her battleground, its nocturnal landscape the setting for her relentless pursuit.

The anonymity of the confessor remained a haunting enigma, a constant question mark at the heart of her investigation. His motives, obscured by a veil of secrecy, remained elusive. Was he a true whistleblower, seeking to atone for his sins? Or was he a puppet, manipulated by others to serve their own ends? The answer held the key to understanding the inner workings of Project Nightingale and preventing future atrocities.

The ending was not a resounding victory, but a stark realization that her fight for justice was far from over. The train journey had concluded, but her personal odyssey, fraught with peril and uncertainty, had only just begun. The weight of choice, the burden of her actions, the relentless pursuit of truth – these were the elements that defined her, shaping her into a warrior against a seemingly insurmountable enemy. The fight, she knew, would continue, a long and arduous battle against a foe that operated in the shadows, its power seemingly limitless. And Ava, armed with her unwavering resolve and the weight of her choices, was ready to face it head-on.

The Philadelphia skyline, once a beacon of hope, now seemed to mock her from afar. The city lights, twinkling like a million distant stars, held no comfort, only a stark reminder of the unfinished battle. The train, a metal serpent that had carried her hopes and fears, had reached its destination, but her journey was far from over. The arrests, the media fanfare, the public pronouncements of justice served – these were mere illusions, carefully crafted to maintain the facade of order in a system deeply riddled with corruption. Project Nightingale, the monstrous conspiracy that had consumed her family, remained a hydra, its many heads severed, yet its body still writhing, its poisonous venom still coursing through the veins of society.

The anonymous confession, a cryptic message delivered from the abyss, haunted her waking hours and invaded her dreams. It was a key, yes, but a key that unlocked not just a door, but a Pandora's Box of secrets, a labyrinth of deception so intricate it threatened to swallow her whole. The confessor's motivations, cloaked in an impenetrable veil of mystery, remained a central enigma. Was he a repentant soul seeking redemption? A double agent playing a deadly game of chess? Or perhaps, a pawn in a larger, even more sinister game? The ambiguity gnawed at her, fueling her relentless pursuit of the truth.

Her allies, a motley crew bound together by shared trauma and a thirst for justice, were as complex as the web of deceit they were fighting. The disillusioned government official, his idealism shattered by years of systemic corruption, offered valuable insights, but his loyalty was always a question mark, his past a minefield of potential betrayals. The disgruntled former employee, scarred by the organization's ruthless efficiency, provided crucial data, but his bitterness often clouded his judgment, his anger a dangerous weapon. And then there was the former rival, a woman whose life had been ravaged by Project Nightingale, her pain fueling a fierce determination to see justice done, yet her ambition sometimes threatened to overshadow their shared goal.

The trust between them was a fragile thing, constantly tested by the betrayals and manipulations that were the very lifeblood of Project Nightingale. The lines of loyalty shifted as readily as the shadows in the city streets, making each interaction a high-stakes gamble, a dance on the razor's edge between cooperation and betrayal. She had learned to read the subtle nuances of human behavior, to decipher the unspoken words, to sense the underlying currents of deceit. Her intuition, honed by years of navigating dangerous situations, became her most trusted advisor, warning her of impending threats, guiding her through treacherous terrain.

The city itself felt like a character in her story, its labyrinthine streets and shadowy alleys mirroring the complexity of the conspiracy. The weight of the city, the weight of her secrets, the weight of her past, pressed down on her, a palpable burden she carried with an unwavering resolve. The city's nocturnal pulse, its hidden life after dark, became the backdrop of her relentless pursuit of the truth. She moved through the city's underbelly like a phantom, disappearing into the shadows, emerging only when necessary, her movements as fluid and silent as a cat stalking its prey.

The digital world offered both a path and a peril. Encrypted messages, coded communications, hidden accounts, offshore corporations, shell companies – these were the building blocks of Project Nightingale's vast empire, a global network designed to launder money and hide its true source of funding. She spent countless nights sifting through mountains of data, painstakingly reconstructing the organization's intricate web of deceit. The sheer volume of information was overwhelming, but her determination never faltered. She was a detective, a warrior, a crusader, fighting against an enemy that seemed invincible, an enemy that operated in the shadows, its tendrils reaching into every corner of society.

The end, when it finally came, was not a triumphant climax, not a satisfying resolution. It was a stark realization that her fight was far from over. Project Nightingale had been wounded, but not destroyed. The individuals she had exposed were merely pawns, readily sacrificed to protect the true architects of the conspiracy. The victory, if it could be called that, was pyrrhic, a momentary reprieve in a long and arduous war. The system, she knew, was self-healing, its inherent corruption too deeply entrenched to be easily eradicated.

The final image lingered in her mind: the empty train carriage, bathed in the cold light of dawn, a silent testament to the struggle that had taken place within its confines. The silence was deafening, broken only by the rhythmic tick-tock of the clock, a relentless reminder of time's relentless march. The passengers, scattered, shaken, their lives irrevocably altered by the events of the journey, were slowly piecing their lives back together. Their stories, intertwined with hers, formed a tapestry of trauma and resilience.

Her personal journey, her quest for justice, had transcended the confines of revenge. It had become a crusade, a battle for a world free from the corrosive influence of corrupt power, a fight for a future where truth and accountability held sway. The weight of her choices, the burden of her actions, the relentless pursuit of justice – these were the elements that defined her, shaping her into a warrior, a symbol of defiance in a world steeped in darkness.

As the sun rose over Philadelphia, casting long shadows across the cityscape, Ava knew that her fight was far from over. The war against Project Nightingale was a marathon, not a sprint. The enemy remained powerful, its reach seemingly limitless. But she, armed with her unwavering resolve, her unwavering commitment to justice, and the knowledge that her fight was a fight for all of us, was ready to continue the battle, a lone warrior in a world desperately in need of heroes. The train had reached its final stop, but her journey, her relentless pursuit of truth, was only just beginning. The final scene faded to black, but the implications resonated long afterward. The final reflection was not one of triumph, but of steely determination, a quiet acknowledgment that the fight had just begun. The epilogue wasn't an ending; it was a beginning.

Project Nightingale: A clandestine, multi-national organization involved in illegal activities, including money laundering, industrial espionage, and political manipulation.

Clean Slate Initiative: A purported philanthropic program used by Project Nightingale as a front for illicit activities.

Phoenix Protocol: Project Nightingale's emergency response plan, designed to eliminate evidence and protect key personnel.

The Labyrinth: A coded network used by Project Nightingale for secure communication.

Seraph: A high-ranking member of Project Nightingale, whose true identity remains unknown.